My Once In A Lifetime

This is a work of fiction. Names, characters, places, and incidents are the products of the author's imagination or are used fictitiously. Any resemblance to actual events, locales, or persons, living or dead, is entirely coincidental.

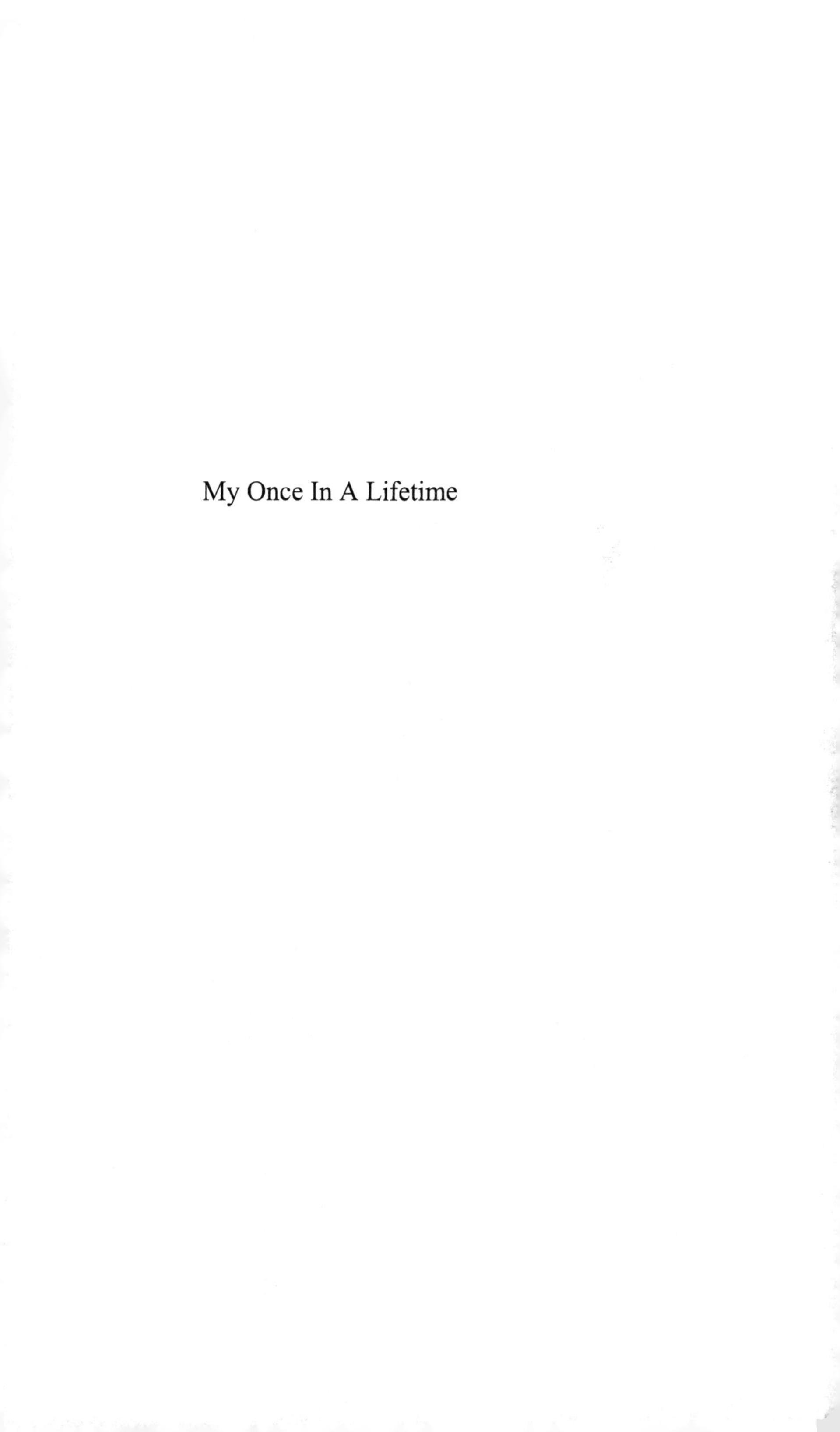

My Once In A Lifetime

Prologue

The crowd inside the bar seemed to be making its way out to the patio. Perfect timing because I needed to restock some supplies, clean glasses and wipe things down. It was a nice little break from the screaming, booze infused people yelling at me for more drinks. Trying to translate their slurred speech was getting to be impossible. Was there such a thing as a Rosetta Stone primary language-intoxication?

I bet I could get a whole pitcher of beer just off the counter. I grabbed a rag and started wiping down the bar counter. Finally, I could hear the band and they were playing one of my favorites, "Tulsa Time" by Don Williams. Getting into my work and singing along I happened to glance up for a quick second over at the booth, kiddie corner from the bar. There was a younger man sitting there in the shadowy corner just staring at me.

I didn't think too much about it as it was not something out of the ordinary and went back to wiping. Something was telling me to look up again. Curious to what my instincts were telling me I squinted back up to that darkly lit booth. Once my eyes adjusted and the dark figure became more clear the hairs on the back of my neck started to stand up and I got a chill down my spine. Our eyes met, he smiled and discretely waved.

Frozen in mid-wipe, I felt myself blankly staring at him in disbelief. He stopped waving at me after about a minute of me standing there not reacting. My mind, heart and body didn't know how to react. Those first two minutes I just stood there, heart pounding so loud it drowned out the music and barely breathing. A small flutter in my stomach flickered only for a millisecond and was quickly crushed as the anger rose threw my entire being like a tsunami. Ryan.

1

Abandonment issues had always been present in my life; from childhood, adolescence to adulthood-it's never faded. I believe there is even a name for what I have-Athazagoraphobia; fear of being forgotten, ignored, or abandoned is a real thing. I Googled it to be sure. Stemming from the death of my father when I was a child, then reappearing with the loss of a best friend in my teenage years therefore; effecting all my future relationships with men.

Just when I thought I had conquered my fear something else would rear its' ugly head back like a twister, obliterating everything internally I had done to heal. My fear causes trust issues in intimate relationships that have tried entering time and time again. I build walls of steel as high as Mt. Everest around my heart certain it would be impenetrable. History has proven nothing is impenetrable; everything has a weakness.

My weakness has always been Ryan. You never really, forget your first true love and in the case, that loves leaves you, you find yourself always comparing others to the first. In your mind, no one other is ever as good as the first. Maybe deep down you know the first was always meant to be and will be. Your heart held out for the first and that is why it could never love another no matter how hard your head fought against it.

Fear made recent events in my life quite trialing. Perseverance and love worked hard to break the stubborn barriers I built inside. The heart knows what the heart wants and it's love that always breaks the spell. Love conquered and burned my fears into ashes that were whisked away in the wind and with that it allowed me to love again.

What caused this fear in me? If he hurt me why did I let him back in? The easiest way to explain everything is to start from the beginning of our story. Love is not easy, it's not always kind, it's not always perfect, love does not always take the same path it did before, but it always finds its' way to the place it is meant to be. Love is what brought him back to me.

2

Two weeks until my senior year at Northfield High School is officially over! Gah! The anticipation for what lies ahead is exhilarating to think about. College, a career, forever home and eventually marriage and a family. *Dream big Ashley, you have a long road ahead*, I thought to myself. The reality of adulthood that is to become me should have me feeling uneasy; college, school loans, debt, job hunting, more debt. Ah, the American dream, though right!?

Back to being a kid while I still can. It's unbelievable how fast my senior year at Northfield High school has gone. My senior year did not go as I had planned, but I will lock it in my good memory bank regardless. Promising myself this year things were going to go my way for once. No holding back, I'm going all out, no-apologies kind of girl, the year of Ashley Monroe!

Shyness is my downfall and has kept me in a shell, branding me as a goodie to shoes. I'm not an introvert by any means it's just I don't feel the need to go out every weekend getting black-out drunk, showing my chest or ass to anyone that will look and making a fool of myself. I drink, I party, I have plenty of friends and have fun. I'm branded as shy because I don't do it the "popular girl" way and because I study my butt off to get good grades.

This was my senior year for heavens sakes and it needs to go down in history as one of the best years of my life. It was time to break out of my comfort zone. I was going to go to parties and get black-out drunk, stay out past curfew, get grounded, skip first period to sleep in because I was up late the night before hanging with Ryan and Brooke; I was going to speak my mind, and dress more like the popular girls in school so more heads will turn my way.

My attire has consisted of leggings, oversized baggy sweatshirts and t-shirts. Nothing about my wardrobe was cute and none of it showed off what God blessed me with; slim figure, great butt and amazing long, dark brown hair. I'm not bragging, but my body is not the worst by any means and if I applied a little makeup to my face -to brighten things up-I might be considered pretty or heck even hot. Most important of all I was going to stop hiding my feelings for my best friend Ryan. Being the best friend of Ryan Black is amazing, but I'm ready to act on my growing feelings and be something more.

I'm sick of being overlooked by him. Seeing all these fake, ditzy, jug heads be in a relationship with Ryan is nauseating. They do not truly appreciate him, as a boyfriend, like I would. To his defense he overlooks me because we have been best friends since the fifth grade and he doesn't know me in any other way. I can't expect to him to read my mind and know how I feel.

Being 18 years old, legally considered an adult, I should know how to use my words to express my thoughts and feelings with others. Like I was saying before, my plans this past summer included; not being a coward, sucking it up and ask Ryan to the homecoming dance. Presenting it to him as, "best friends owing it to each other to have a good time and dancing the night away together." I decided not to overwhelm him all at once in the beginning of the year with my confession. Slowly and subtly put signs out there would be a better approach.

Being more physical like touching his arm, longer hugs, laughing at his dumb boy jokes and behaviors, hanging out more just the two of us and then eventually by mid to the end of the year I would tell him how I feel. Not wanting to seem eager to ask him to the dance the first week of school, I decided waiting until the second week would suffice. Since I'm easy to blush, asking him was not going to be some big elaborate production with signs and balloons or some crazy YouTube video like the others do. When we were hanging out, just the two of us, is when I would do it.

It seemed like a good plan, my ducks were in a row for him to be all mine. Nope! None of it went as planned. Thanksgiving and Christmas briskly came and went, still dressing in lounge wear at school. A hand full of times throughout the whole year I dressed in the latest styles that girls wearing.

As for being laid back and letting loose-not so much. I was still going to a few parties here and there, but more often than not I was hunkering down studying as I always had throughout my years in school. Before I knew it, prom was here. After prom, I blinked and now here's graduation staring us straight in the face. The execution of my plan, "Make Ryan Mine" most definitely, did not go as planned either.

There was always an excuse as to why now was not the best time. The times I would talk myself into being more physical with him or asking him to the dance there was another girl in the way; my timing is always the worst. The year of Ashley Monroe has been a failure. I lived through this year just as I had the years before; plain, uneventful and not intimately any closer to Ryan. It didn't matter though, as our post high school plans were in the horizon.

The California sun and a new life with my two best friends was fast approaching. Our junior year Ryan, Brooke and myself made-a-plan to move out to California together and get away from the small-town life we were living in. Northfield, Minnesota is the picture-perfect river town that most people dream of living in to raise their families, but being 18 years old I'm nowhere near that stage in life and want out. I'm looking for excitement, adventure, culture, the big city life! For a town with a motto of "Cows, Colleges, and Contentment" you can only imagine how exciting things get around here. Oh, that's right they don't! Don't get me wrong I love my hometown, but this girl is busting at the seams to see the world; well at least for now seeing the west coast.

With having two colleges in town you think this would be the hippest place around and full of action all the time; it's the farthest from that at least in my opinion. The main event that the whole town looks forward to all year is *The Defeat of Jesse James Days.* Yes, our town is known for an attempted robbery on the First National Bank of Northfield by Jesse James and the James-Younger Gang in which local citizens resisted the robbers and thwarted the theft. It's quite a big deal and a whole weekend is dedicated to it. It is a pretty cool weekend and part of the town's heritage.

I don't regret growing up here, it's your typical Midwestern farming town filled with boutiques, shops and river walkways and Ryan. UCLA had an amazing nursing school program that I had my eye on and that's how we decided upon moving out to California. It also aligned with Ryan's dreams of becoming an actor and Brooke was going along because she didn't have any concrete plan and well, why not?!

The thought of the unknown is so exhilarating. Soon I will be far away from the frigid Minnesota winters but, I'm going to miss this little college river town. It has been such an amazing place to grow up in, but I'm ready to move on to bigger and better things. We will be on our own in sunny California, trying to make our mark in the world out there.

As I said Ryan wants live out the so called "American Dream" and break onto the big screen. His idea of the American dream and mine are two different things. He loves to be the center of attention while I like when it's just the three of us hanging out with no one else around. He loves the attention he gets from girls and how every guy wants to be his friend. The girls are drawn to Ryan as he is your tall, dark and handsome type. He is built just right, if you ask me; 6'4", slightly toned, just enough muscle. Ryan also carries those Midwestern qualities that are added perks to his good looks; well mannered, great sense of humor and a hard work ethic.

He knows how to make a girl feel like she's the only one in the room and he knows how to work those dark brown eyes and flawless smile. That charm, manners and good looks is what draws you into him. Once you are roped there's no turning back. I on the other hand know how he works it with the ladies and I'm immune to his spell. Or so I thought.

Don't get me wrong even as my best friend that smile has grown on me and gives me the butterflies every time he is near me, but I've learned to control those feelings only until recently. I have known Ryan since we were in the fifth grade. We have spent most of our lives together as neighbors, but most importantly best of friends. I noticed through our adolescent years it was becoming increasingly harder to resist Ryan. The feeling of wanting more than just a best friend relationship was overcoming me.

It doesn't help that since high school I wasn't receiving his undivided attention any more like I used which made me want him all-the-more. It was a challenge to me. His attention was routed towards a good quarter or more of the female population at Northfield High School. Another fifty percent to the hockey team, the last quarter devoted to his studies and myself when his social life allowed.

Brooke Smith, my other long-time friend since middle school is what I would call a free spirit; doesn't yet know what she wants to do with her life so she plans to waitress tables and live off tips until she figures life out. Long blonde, short stature, slim and toned, good looking, awesome personality and an adventurous spirit. As far as California goes, guess you could just say she's along for the ride with Ryan and I. One plan she does have for herself is to backpack every trail possible in America-more of a bucket list item and do yoga all the time. Brooke has a calm about her that winds you down when you are all worked up or in a tense situation.

She is great to have around. "Live life to the fullest and free of worry," is her motto. Needless, to say she is full of amazing qualities and beauty and has no issues attracting guys.

I on the other hand, I did have a well-drawn out plan after high school. I'm the organized, like to have my ducks in a row, planner type unlike Brooke who just lives day to day. I was accepted into the UCLA School of Nursing this past fall. I want to get my RN licensure and work in labor and delivery. I shadowed an OB/GYN nurse during one of my college career classes and fell in love with this area of patient care.

I knew immediately, without a doubt it's what I wanted to do with my life. I had scoped out UCLA a year and a half prior with my mother. I fell in love with the school and surrounding area. With the dense population, there was sure to be job opportunities in my field once I graduated. I would have to spend my first two years of college living in the dorms, which completely bummed me out, as I wanted to room with Ryan and Brooke in an apartment.

I tried to look at the bright side of it though and accepted that initially living on my own would also help keep me on the straight and narrow to stay focused on my studies. As much as I love those two they have never been quite as serious and focused on their studies as I have. In the long run not living with them for would turn out to be a positive thing and the right decision.

Monday morning, Ryan and I were out in the front of the school basking in the warm spring sun, waiting for the warning bell to ring. I looked over at him, just admiring his dark black hair and that defined face. I couldn't get enough, looking at him made me melt. I loved when I could see his jaw bones tensing up. He must have felt me looking at him because then his charming smile spread across his face and he looked over at me, "What?!"

I chuckled and shrugged, "Oh nothing, just admiring that zit coming in on your cheek."

"What, are you kidding me?" as he started feeling up his face in a panic.

I giggled again knowing I was under his skin, as he hates anything, foreign living on that perfect skin of his.

"Oh chill out, I'm kidding. I just know how upset you get thinking something is growing on your perfect little face and I just wanted to get rise out of you. You know, get that blood pressure going before a full day of classes start."

"Always the comedian", he said as he swung his toned arm around me and walked me into school.

As much as I like to think that his arm around my shoulders is going to make the other girls jealous in school I know that to not be the truth. Most of the girls that have grown up in this town know Ryan has me in "that" category that does not threaten them, it has been that way since childhood.

Walking down the bustling hallways as everyone is running to get to their classes on time, I thought about how I am going to miss high school and all that goes with it; chatting with friends in the hallways and in class, the never-ending lectures from teachers, the smells (yes the smells), pep rallies, football games, school dances, working at the barn with my girlfriends, late night parties at the grove. I guaranteed myself adulthood will be just as great. I'm looking forward to what life has planned for me.

Sitting in history class listening to Mr. Mesnik explain what our final test is going to consist of was starting to bore me. I couldn't help but start to daydream of what life in California is going to be like. California daydreams have completely consumed my mind for many months now which is not like me to not be focused in class. Focusing in on studies with only two weeks of class left has proven to be difficult. I reassured myself it would be okay since I have worked my butt off these past four years and have another four more years of hard work ahead of me.

My daily daydreams consisted of weekends at the beach, morning coffee with Ryan and Brooke, the shopping…. then my dream bubble popped when Krista kept whispering my name "Ashley, hey Ashley."

"Huh, what's up?" I mumbled and a little annoyed my daydream was interrupted.

"So are you guys actually going to go through with leaving home and moving out to California so soon after graduation?"

"Heck yes, why wouldn't we?" I said.

"It's just so far from home. You don't know anyone out there. Have you ever been so far away from your mom and brother?"

"No and it will be hard, but I have to do it. I NEED to get out of this town and make something of myself. There is nothing for me here."

As I said this I felt guilt; guilt that I was leaving my mom behind with my little brother. I need to go and there's no turning back. It's potentially only for the next four to five years that I will be away from them. We will call and Skype every day, it will be like I never left. Plus, my biggest concern is letting Ryan know how I feel about him. For me that is just as important as going to school for nursing.

After Mr. Mesnik was done outlining what the final test would entail, the rest of the period he allowed for study time. Most of the study time was spent talking with Krista and hashing out each of our plans after graduation. She was staying in town and attending a local college in town, Carleton College, but had no idea what she wanted to major in. Krista's concentration would not be on her studies or narrowing down what to major in, but college guys and all the parties she planned to attend. My plans entailed studying my butt off to get through college, clinicals, landing a job and starting a life with Ryan. That is, if Ryan would have me and my big plans for a life together.

This is the happy path that I have planned for my life. There is no room or time to divert from these plans.

I look forward to fourth period study hall everyday with Ryan and Brooke because this is when we do all our planning for our move out west. The first three class periods of day absolutely kill me with boredom as Dr. Time goes by ever so slowly. History, Photography, English and then Study Hall!! I'm so over school right now as are most of my class mates. Finally, fourth period!

I headed to the cafeteria where study hall took place and found Ryan and Brooke sitting there talking about the latest drama at Northfield High. I walked up on the tail end of their conversation to hear Brooke saying to Ryan, "So you told her no, right?"

Throwing my bag on the table I said, "Told who no?"

"Oh just the same ol' Mr. Black playing the dating game. Little Ms. Miranda Stolz asked Ryan if he would go with her to the after-graduation party at The Grove." Brook said laughing.

He chuckled and looked up at me and as he did I rolled my eyes and gave him a look of pure irritation. He knows that as his best friend I disapprove of his string of flings. I've told him time and time again that he can do better, that he deserves better. As any typical high school guy, does, he's packing as much fun in as he can especially in his senior year. Depending on who his latest fling is we normally just crack jokes about the girls and the dates they go on. But, every now and then he will go on a streak of keeping the same girl around for more than three weeks.

There's a part of me that does start to worry that this girl might stick, which then my irritation shines through and I take it out on Brooke and Ryan. When I get like that they chalk it up to my time of the month. Pure jealousy and worry on my part. I worry that this one "fling" just might get serious and I will never have the chance to tell him how I feel. Never wanting to regret anything in my life; not telling him my true feelings would be the ultimate regret.

Enough of this irritating conversation, time to move on to more productive conversations.

"So moving on, did you two come across any leads for jobs yet?"

"Jobs Ash, I'm jumping right into auditions. I'm not wasting one moment out there with anything else."

"Ryan, really?! Do you think your apartment, food and spending money pays for itself?"

"Chill out Ashley, my parents are going to be paying for my first six months out there until I can get on my feet."

I wish I had the luxury of two parents that were comfortable financially, like his, to take care of me while I'm away at school. I needed to get of out of this slump of a mood and be happy for him that finances would not be a burden for him, at least not right away.

"Oh, that's awesome! What a relief for you."

"Yes I thought so too." Ryan said.

"So how about you Brooke? Any jobs lined up?" I asked.

"Actually, I do have a waitressing job lined up. My mom's best friend runs an Italian restaurant out in the Brentwood area and they just lost a few waitresses and said it was perfect timing for me to join. I start a week after we get out there, so we will have a few days to move in and scope out the beaches and guys Ash." As she playfully giggled at her big plans the first week we are out there.

"How about that Ryan, you up for scoping out guys on the beach?" as I playfully nudged his arm.

"Pretty sure I'm up for scoping out ladies with long legs and bikinis."

The thought of him with a California babe, made me sick to my stomach. There can't be any other girls interrupting my plans to be with him. My plan is to give it a few weeks and get settled in before I confess my feelings for him, but maybe just after a week wouldn't be so bad. Telling him sooner would allow us more time to build our relationship before I start in with school. I know I'm in panic mode, but how could I not be.

I have been patiently waiting for him the last two years of high school. I decided at the beginning of our senior year it would be my time after graduation.

Ryan and I have been best friends since the fifth grade. That is when my family moved next door to his family on Maple Lane. I was sitting on the front lawn that summer reading a book, *I Am the Ice Worm*. This was my favorite book in my youth as I could relate to it in many ways, with the exception mine was surrounding the death of my father not a plane crash. Abandonment do to a tragedy, survival and learning to adapt to different surroundings because of the tragedy.

So, I was there reading in the yard when there he was, walking right up to me. There was no hesitation from him to come talk to me. Most fifth-grade boys still believe in koodies.

Even in fifth grade that kid had a certain swagger and charm about him. I remember it was a perfect, hot and humid, summer day, he asked if I wanted to ride my bike down to the park. I had not made any friends yet, as school had not yet resumed from summer break and we had just moved to town. I was so excited to have someone to play with that I didn't care if it was boy or a girl. I dropped my book right where I was sitting, jumped up smiling and ran into the house to ask my mom permission to go with him.

Since that fine summer day, we have been inseparable. I couldn't have asked for a better beginning to our story. It was not until the beginning of our sophomore year in high school that something changed and I began to develop more than "just friends" feelings for him.

The summer after our freshman year is when Ryan hit puberty and bulked up. His spurt into manhood, I can guarantee is what spiked his popularity with the girls and guys at school. His role on the hockey team grew due to his immense skill set and natural talent on the ice, he started dating often and was attending more and more high school parties every weekend. He was even invited to parties by juniors and seniors at the time.

Our junior year, one of those so-called flings turned serious with Katie Cam. His time for me had shortened; this is when the flame ignited in me. I noticed how amazing he was in this new relationship. He gave her every ounce of his attention, opened the car door for her, held her hand, hugged her, breathed her in with every little kiss, treated her to surprise dates and presents. During their long (to me), seven-month relationship I came second in his life and I hated it.

I was only good enough to be around when Katie was not around or not available for him to drool over. I hated every day, every minute and second of this relationship, all one hundred and eighty-three days, four thousand three hundred ninety-two hours, two hundred sixty-three thousand five hundred and twenty minutes and fifteen million eight hundred eleven thousand and two hundred seconds of it. Pathetic, yes I know. Although he was my friend and I did truly want him to be happy I came to the realization that I wanted him to be happy with me. I know him the best inside and out, his like and dislikes.

Once I figured out why I was struggling with his relationship with Katie, I decided that as soon as they broke up, if they ever did, I would let him know my feelings for him. Right before the end of our junior year Katie and Ryan did break up. He seemed down about the break up for all of one week and then he was back to his old ways of speed dating. At least I had his attention back. We were back to being Ryan and Ashley, best friends.

I didn't want to seem eager since his relationship with Katie had just ended, even though I was jumping out of my skin to tell him, but I figured I would give it at least a few weeks before I would profess my feelings for him. Those "few weeks" ended up turning into months, since their breakup was at a time full of finals, start- up of summer jobs and college visits. I had become so busy with the business of summer that I had kind of put telling him on the back burner. Don't get me wrong I still felt the same way about him and had always worried he would get into another relationship and I would lose my chance, but I was enjoying the moment being friends. Part of the reason I had not told him was that I could not work up the courage to tell him.

I would freeze every time I thought I had the guts to tell him or the opportunity just wasn't there because Brooke was around or the timing and place was just not right.

Then we had come up with our brilliant plan to move out west. I made a promise to myself that I would tell him once we got out there regardless if he was in a relationship back home or not. I was going to be selfish for once and do what was right for me. This was still the year of Ashley Monroe.

Fourth period class ended with the release bell for lunch. We continued with the monotonous daily school routine. I grew bored of this routine fast these last few weeks, but I tried not to take it for granted as I knew life was currently easy and I would want to be back in this moment. In the next few days to come all the seniors were buckling down, studying for finals, starting summer jobs, making last minute preparations for graduation ceremony and graduation parties. Unfortunately, Brooke, Ryan and I would not be attending any of our classmate's grad parties as were leaving the day after graduation for California.

One thing that we did plan to attend was the unofficial senior class party at The Grove right after the ceremony. The Grove is a place for just us teens to be able to relax, kick back listening to music, and where we partied all year long. This would be our last time to reminisce about all the good times, breathe in the last few breaths of that fresh country air, enjoy the last few moments of our adolescent years, while having a few underage drinks and say our goodbyes to everyone we have grown up with most of our lives.

3

Three days before graduation! I could taste that sweet California sun. Its warmth kissing my cheeks and tanning my pale Minnesota skin. I could not help but think to myself that life could not get much better than this. I only had one final left this week and the remaining school days were only half days. For only being half days they sure did drag on.

Kids were getting restless sitting in class at this point in the year. The teachers were doing all that they could to keep our attention. Most kids were out of the classroom doors before the first second of the bell was even done dinging. I had such a jam-packed week ahead. I feel like I barely have time to blink let alone doing anything else that I had planned.

Tonight, consisted of studying for my last final of the week-if I could spare enough attention to do so-then packing up my room, finishing up my last shifts at The Red Barn and spending what time I had left with my mom and little brother Charlie. This past Sunday I spent the entire day with my brother and mom. We cooked breakfast together at home as we did every Sunday, but this time we added to our menu. Typically, we cooked eggs with cheese and salsa and bacon, but since it was my last breakfast at home we added pancakes and fruit. Then we went for a hike at the Nerstrand Big Woods State Park and avoided talking about me leaving in a few days, as it always made my mom weepy.

It was so refreshing to be with them. Just the three of us, as it had been the past nine years. We spent the day as if nothing big was about to happen or change in any of our lives.

Wrapping up the day with a last-minute barbeque with Ryan and his family. Venison steaks, baked potatoes and green beans were on the menu. My favorite childhood meal. I grew up on this stuff and would not have it any other way. Ryan's dad made a mean venison steak. My mouth waters thinking of it. It was great to spend my last few hours with these amazing people. The Black family has been as close to me as my own blood family. I had spent many hours over at the Black household. Great down to earth, hardworking people. I respected and looked up to them and would miss them greatly.

After dinner and chit chatting, I helped clean up and then said my good bye for the night as I promised myself I would dedicate at least two hours to studying for my very last high school history final. I got home and sat at my desk in my bedroom, opened my history text book and study notes. My concentration broke after fifteen minutes of my "dedicated study time"; my mind was consumed with all that I had to do and all that would be happening in the days ahead. I tried stretching it out for a few more minutes, but decided it was useless and went downstairs to join in watching a Sunday night movie with the family. I didn't worry too much about studying for my final as I was confident in the topics that we would be tested on. I have always been good in that subject.

I snuggled up to my mom on the couch with some popcorn and movie. I would miss my little family greatly and was so thankful for the day that I spent with them and all that we did together. Sundays nights would be different without them.

Beep, beep, beep, beep!! 6:45 am and the sound of my alarm came way too quickly. I was a little groggy from staying up past eleven last night to finish out the movie. I hit snooze too many times to count and before I knew it I only had fifteen minutes to get ready and out the door to school. I threw a pair of black leggings on with a white Minnesota Twins shirt, threw my hair up in a messy bun, grabbed a banana and yogurt to go for breakfast and bolted out the door as my mom was yelling out the door to me "Good luck!"

Arriving to school, on my last Monday as a senior is bittersweet. Feeling a little teary eyed thinking about it. There was no time to reminisce about it now, I was two minutes away from being late to class and sprinted towards the front doors. Barely saved by the bell I slide into Mr. Mesnik's history class just as he was shutting the door. He didn't waste any time in giving us our finals. It was right to business as he plopped them down onto each of our desks.

As I started going through the test and filling in the little ovals, I looked around at my fellow-classmate's observing their panicked yet determined looks on their faces as they hurried through their tests. It took me all of twenty minutes to finish. We were instructed to bring our tests to the front basket on Mr. Mesnik's desk so he could begin to correct and score. The remainder of class was to be spent in silence so all students could finish their tests.

As the end of the period bell rang, Mr. Mesnik yelled out the door that our final scores and grades for the year would be posted on the school portal and wished us all the best of luck at the graduating ceremony. All I had left for my half day was photography and that final class just consisted of cleaning all the film processing tools and then screwing around the remainder of the hour. It was a waste of our time if you ask me. Why can't they just let us out even earlier? Just an excuse to torture us for one last time.

When photography class ended, I didn't spend much time in the hallways to stop and talk with friends as I had to stay on task-moving day was only two days away and tonight I had my last shift at The Red Barn. So, there was minimal time in between leaving school and going to work that I had for some last-minute packing. I headed out to my car, keeping my head down as to not make eye contact with anyone so that I wouldn't get stopped for pointless conversations.

When I got home, and walked into the house my big plans to finish up all packing was interrupted by my mom asking me to do a few chores around the house and my brother Charlie wanting to throw the baseball around in the backyard. I didn't have the heart to turn him down as I wanted to make it a point to spend as much time with him as I could. Plus, I had not seen my mother and him a whole lot these past few weeks as we had all been so busy with our own schedules.

My time was consumed with studying for finals and working at the barn for extra cash. Mom's time was spent working like crazy, taking my brother to his doctor's appointments, baseball practices and games. I like to think that he might get a little lonely without me when I leave. *What are him and mom going to do without me here*, I thought to myself? I figured I would leave myself an hour before work to pack and then finish up what I had left tomorrow.

Throwing the ball around in the backyard with Charlie had a special place in my heart and is one request I had a hard time saying no to. This was one of the great memories I had of my dad and I, that we did together often before he passed. My little freckled faced brother Charlie was eight years younger than me and my true best friend next to Ryan. He was such a warm hearted, funny little guy that could always get me out of a gray mood and comforted me when I needed it. Charlie and I have been through a lot together.

I guess you could say I helped raise him as my dad passed not long after he was born from a heart attack eight winters ago while shoveling the driveway. Unfortunately, none of us were home when it happened. The neighbor found him lying in the snowbank next to the drive way and by then it was too late. My father was a perfectly healthy guy, so the fact that he died by a heart attack was devastating. My mother, with a newborn baby and an eight-year old girl, was now left to raise the both of us on her own. She told me a few years ago, it was hard for her to grasp the reality of it all and for the longest time she expected him to walk right back in that front door from shoveling the driveway. Reality can be hard to accept.

The hard road she had ahead of her was hard to swallow, but she always tried to do it with her head held high. It took her a while to figure out how she was going to raise two young kids on a single income, but like I said she somehow did it. Granted she had his life insurance money to get her through most of the first year and a half, but as that dwindled down she knew she would have to ask for more full-time work at the hospital in town where she worked as a nurse on the medical/surgical floor. She wanted to make sure that we lived comfortably and be able to have the things most kids our age had, but within reason.

Being eight years old at the time when this all happened I tried to help-out the best I could. Whether it was doing the dishes or feeding Charlie his bottle. I figured anything could help her out even if it was the smallest thing. My mother is a strong woman and she really, pushed through her own emotions and the hard times and gave us the best that she could with what she had.

I internally struggled with the loss of my dad. Many nights I would cry because I missed him so much. Other nights I even found myself angry at my deceased father for whatever reason. I didn't know why the anger was there, but I think it stemmed from feeling abandoned by him. My heart knew that wasn't the real case, but my head struggled to think otherwise.

When you only have one parent, you think about the things you took for granted when you did have two. My worries might have seemed miniscule to others, but they still meant something to me. I didn't have that other parent to go to, to ask for a treat when originally mom was the first one to say no; no daddy daughter dances, no softball coach, wrestling matches on the living room floor, my knight and shining armor. I missed the one on one time playing catch with him in the backyard. Most of all I missed the love of father.

It's different kind of love than a mother's love. The love a father gives you, is one you try to look for in your relationships with boyfriends and spouses and aspire to have. I tried not to be too emotional about it in front of my mom as I wanted to be strong for her. I didn't want to put her under more stress than she already was under. She never expressed her stress or frustrations about the hand she had been dealt, but I could always tell. The dark circles and bags under her eyes. Regardless of those minor blemishes she is still always the most beautiful mom to me.

As Charlie and I continued to throw the old ratted out baseball around the backyard he said, “Ashley, are you coming with mom and I to my doctor’s appointment this afternoon?”

“Sorry buddy, I really would come, but I have to work. But you call me as soon as you are finished there and tell me all about it.”

“Oh okay.” he said with a tinge of disappointment.

Charlie had been complaining of severe leg pain the past few weeks and they have been trying to pin point the cause of it. The pain has been getting so bad for him lately that he has begun to walk with a little limp. The end of last week he was up at Children’s Hospital doing blood and imaging tests. We have all been a little worried about him of course, but I haven’t thought twice about it and just figured he stress fractured his leg at baseball practice or something.

“Hey mom”, I walked towards the kitchen to where she was sitting sorting out bills.

“Yes ma’am what can I help you with today?”

“Can you please call me after Charlie’s appointment or text me and let me know how it all went so I’m not worrying the whole time I’m at work?”

“Sure thing, what time will you be home?”

“My shift ends at ten tonight and I will be home soon after.”

“So what is my big graduating girl’s plan for her last few days of school?” she asked a little teary eyed.

I knew she was thinking about dad at this point because any milestones either of us kids made she would always comment how our dad would be so proud, but he is watching us from above.

"Well this is my last night to work at the barn. Tomorrow is my last exam, Wednesday morning is our run through of the graduation ceremony, in the evening is actual graduation and after the ceremony we have the unofficial senior party, and then Thursday we are off to California!"

"Oh sweetie, I'm so proud of you and I know your dad is too" as she started to break down. "You have just been so amazing through everything and you are such a good kid. I can't wait to see what the next chapter in your life will bring although, we will miss you greatly back here at home. You have to promise Charlie and me that you will call, text, or Skype a minimum of every other day."

"Yes mom, of course I will. It will be like I never left."

We hugged out the rest of her breakdown, she kissed me on my head as she always does with a squeeze and we were off on our separate ways for the afternoon.

.

4

I snatched up some last-minute shifts at The Red Barn here in Northfield. It was a seasonal joint that baked pizza, hosted weddings and other events at this beautiful rustic country barn. They had picnic tables indoors and out, a lot of people also ate their pizza picnic style on the grass on a blanket.

Driving to work with the windows rolled down, breathing in every ounce of country air that I could. The smell of fresh cut grass, the putrid smell of fertilizer spread amongst the country fields, the smell of the Malt O Meal plant, the sound of the Canon River rolling by as I passed driving to work or even walking through town. All these smells and scenes from living in a small town, one does take it for granted, but typically, you don't notice how much you miss it until you are away from them. I pulled into the gravel driveway at work and it was a bittersweet feeling. I was glad to be done working, but I would miss all my co-workers, customers and the big red barn itself.

This place gave off such a friendly, hometown feeling that anyone would miss. I walked in and saw Brooke already spreading the toppings over the first set of pizzas. I threw on my apron and dived right into helping her. Every little piece of pepperoni, sausage and mushroom I placed with heart and tactfulness. I wanted these to be the best, last pizzas I made for our customers. Normally, I wouldn't take this much pride in the placement of the condiments, but I was in such a great mood that I couldn't wipe the smile off my face.

Usually, I spend the first hour prepping the pizzas to bake, then the next half hour is spent prepping the dining area for those that sit indoors and then running around like a chicken with its head cut-off once the customers start lining up to get fresh pizzas and making sure there is enough utensils. As all of us girls were prepping the pizzas, a co-worker/school mate-that I'm not necessarily too fond of-Tasha Jennings, asked all of us if we had heard that Miranda asked Ryan to go to the senior party with her at the Grove tomorrow night. Irritation began to rise, but I tried pushing back inside. I pretended to act like I had not heard this conversation going on and went about my work, but of course they dragged me right back into it.

"Hey Ashley, so do you know what he ended up saying to Miranda?" as all of them were staring at me, intensely waiting for an answer.

Why do they feel the need to ask me anything and everything about Ryan's life? They act like I knew it all, which I pretty much do, but certainly do not need to share those details with them. Miranda has been pursuing Ryan pretty much the entire senior year. They have been on a few dates and been to the Grove a few times together, but Ryan had tried to avoid making anything official with anyone before leaving for California. He wanted to spend his senior year free of commitment and ties that come with a relationship.

He just wanted to have fun. Miranda has been determined to break this idea he had in his head, obviously, right up to the very end. Turning to face them with the biggest eye roll I had ever given and attitude I said,

"How the heck would I know? I don't keep track of his dating schedule."

I turned back around to the pizzas and at this point I was throwing toppings down, no longer with heart and tactfulness. My irritation was being taken out on the toppings. I don't know why I was letting this conversation get me so upset. What was there to worry about? He would be all mine in less than a day.

Part of my distress was I had imagined the perfect graduation day and the perfect after party together. Ryan and I would hang out the entire time together saying goodbye to everyone under the stars, throwing back some cold ones like we always have. One last high school party together. Miranda asking him to go with her was ruining all my plans, which I of course hate since I like everything to go as planned. I peered over to Brooke who was looking back at me with a smile and just shook her head at me and turned to the girl's and told them;

"He did mention to me that he told her that he didn't want to be tied down with a date there, but that they could meet up at the party and hang out together."

They all giggled and gossiped about this news. Any of Ryan's activities were always hot gossip. After about five minutes of clucking like hens they all finally got back to work and I began to feel myself calm down. The first round of pizzas were about ten minutes away from coming out of the oven when the owner, Mr. Simon, burst through the door and said,

"Alright, alright, alright, all my hardworking kids, doors open in five, so everyone please man your battle stations."

I loved my boss, his laid-back style of management and the way he incorporates fun into a job. I only hoped I would have bosses as great as him down the road. Mr. Simon walked over to Brooke and me, wrapping both his arms around us, gave a squeeze.

"Girls, I'm going to miss my two hardest workers in this joint, not sure we can stay afloat without you. Are you sure you don't want to stay?"

"As tempting as this sounds Mr. Simon, I'm okay with looking out my window each day to see waves and surfers, not fields and cows." said Brooke.

"Gee I would stay, but school is already lined up for me out there, but thanks Mr. Simon for keeping me on all these years. You are the best of the best!"

"Well, Ashley I was not expecting such a compliment and thank you! That means so much to me. Wish the rest of our crew had work ethic like Brooke and yourself. Enough of all this fluffy sentimental stuff, let's open the doors and serve up some dough."

There was never a moment of down time so shifts at the barn always flew by. I could feel my phone buzzing in my pocket and figured it was my mother calling about my brother's appointment. Everyone in town was here eating tonight I swear it. There was no way I had the time to answer her call. I didn't think twice about answering it as I knew she would just tell me whatever it was she had to say about Charlie's appointment in the morning.

During the season the barn was open, pizza nights were always crazy busy and summer weekends were always filled with weddings or other events. On pizza night's there was room inside the barn for customers to sit, but we always promoted outdoor picnic style seating on a blanket to get the full enjoyment of the summer weather, delicious pizza and wine if they so choose to. The grounds are lit with porch and globe string lighting to give it a romantic touch. Working weddings were my favorite event. Seeing the couple's romantic and fairy tale day unfold was amazing. It gave me butterflies every time.

The dresses, decorations, flowers and the first dance with the low lighting was my favorite. I always daydreamed about the day that I get to be in the bride's shoes.

As I was walking a pizza order out to a couple sitting on a flannel blanket a few yards from the barn I caught a glimpse of Ryan and his brute gang of friends walking up. He gave me a wave and a smile. I smiled and waved back as we walked towards each other.

"Are you sure you aren't going to miss the summer sweat and marinara sauce all over you Ash? Don't get me wrong it is a good look on you." as he tugged on my marina splattered apron. "You could probably make a career out of this if you wanted. You know Mr. Simon would keep you in a heartbeat."

I felt myself blushing a bit.

"Yeah, yeah very funny Ryan." as I started to walk back to the barn.

"Somebody has to keep you in line in California. Your usual order will be out shortly.", I shouted back at him.

Ryan and his friends came out for pizza almost every Monday night, especially in the summers. Needless, to say it was always an eventful shift when they came in. Distracting all the workers, mostly the girls of course and they were loud, obnoxious and messy. Boys will be boys.

Four tiring hours later, my last shift ended at the barn. Everything was cleaned up and restocked for the next night. I hugged all my co-workers, even the one's I didn't like and thanked Mr. Simon repeatedly for the last four years he's employed me here. Leaving there with a smile on my face and great memories. The windows were down as I drove home on this warm summer night.

I blasted my favorite country station, 107.9 Bob FM, and sung my heart out like I was in the shower. This was my way of unwinding after the night's shift before my long study night ahead. I had my last final at school tomorrow and then I was a free woman.

5

The morning alarm went off before I knew it. I feel like my head had just had hit my pillow. I was up until about one in the morning doing some crash course studying. I tried not to stress too much about studying for my finals as I had good standing grades and knew this was not a make or break test for me, but I still wanted to do well as this was my last high school exam I would ever take. I felt like a Mack truck had hit me though and knew it would be a several cups of coffee kind of day.

Between working last night, the stress of these last few days of school and studying I knew I had not been getting good quality sleep. I would have to make up for the lost hours of sleep once we arrived in California and got settled in. I threw on some jeans and a cute loose fitting stripped shirt, left my hair down with no makeup and ran down the stairs to grab a cup of coffee to go. Hair styling and cute outfits to school had been lacking these past few weeks. I couldn't put forth the energy into getting all dolled up every day when there was so many other things going on.

I stepped out onto the front stoup and breathed in the brisk morning air. Minnesota summer mornings were the best and I loved them. The bright sunrise, smell of fresh cut grass, the smell of the previous night's bonfire smoldering and birds chirping. Sounds cliché, but I don't care I still love it and will miss it. I jogged towards my car, started up the Escort and turned on the heat and defrost. Although it was nearly summer, the mornings were still brisk and cool. I waited a few minutes for the windshield to be clear of the fog and started my last official ride into high school.

I pulled into my usual parking spot, grabbed my backpack and headed in. As I opened the doors into school the familiar sounds of clanking locker doors, giggling girls and loud boys flooded my ears. It made me smile, but I had no time to stop and join in on the chattered as I only had one minute to spare before I had to be in science class. I stepped into science class and tried to stop breathing all together as I hated the smell of that room. It always smelled of formaldehyde, bleach, harsh hand soap, mixed with rich metallic undertones and hints of pencil erasers.

I sat my butt in the chair right as the bell rang. I was eager to get this test started and leave school for good. I had so much to do-like always-before graduation tomorrow. Mr. Cue started placing the tests on each student's desks right when the bell rang and said we could start right away and leave when we were done. Although, I had an A in this class I had to work hard in science as this subject did not come easy for me.

It took me almost twenty-five minutes to finish the test, but I did and I felt good about what my ending score would be. I grabbed my backpack, walked silently up to Mr. Cue's desk and placed my test in his wire basket and walked out the door. I walked down the hall to my locker to clean out the last few pictures and trinkets I had left in there. When I opened my locker the collage of memories flooded my eyes; parties we attended over the last four years of school, selfies of Ryan and I, football and hockey games and school dances. So many great memories we have made over the years.

I can't wait to make even more with these amazing people I call my best friends. I took these frozen in time memories and put them into my bag and then cleaned out the rest of my locker which contained random remnants that went straight into the garbage. I looked up and down the hallways which only had a few kids out and about roaming as I'm assuming most others were finishing up their exams. I was anxious to get home and finish up things so I decided not to stick around to wait for everyone to get out. I was on a mission to get my list of stuff done by tonight so I don't need to worry about it before I leave.

I drove onto the driveway and headed into the house as I was making a mental note of all that I needed to get done. I was determined to wrap up everything as I knew my brother and mom would be gone most of the day at school and working. When I walked into the house I turned my phone off and had tunnel vision for the missions that needed to be completed. I packed my carry-on bag for the airport minus the toiletries I needed the next morning, got my graduation outfit ready, and packed up the last of my room. I felt a load stress come off my back having got this done.

I wanted to help my mom with things around the house to help make the initial transition of me being gone smooth; I decided to make her some freezer meals. We didn't have all the ingredients that I needed so I ran to the grocery store and stocked up on supplies for my meals and extra things for her to have. In two hour's I knocked out a few days' worth of dinners for her; tater tot hot dish, lasagna and beef stroganoff. It wasn't much, but I knew it would help her out and she would appreciate it. After cleaning my kitchen mess up, I started with the rest of the house and cleaned the bathrooms, vacuumed and dusted.

With my busy afternoon, I forgot to feed my growling stomach so I made myself a salad and sat down at the counter to eat. As soon as I sat down to eat, Charlie and mom walked in the door. Charlie came in and grabbed a snack and went straight to the television to watch cartoons. My mom walked in with a distraught look on her face and puffy red eyes like she had been crying. I just assumed the thought of me graduating and leaving in the next few days was really, getting to her, but still concerned I asked if she was doing okay?

She had stopped herself at the counter, dropped her purse to the floor and started bawling. I walked right over to her and chuckled a bit and started rubbing her back for comfort and said,

"Mom, it's really going to be fine. I promise I will call often and visit home when I can."

At that moment when she looked up at me, I knew that she was not crying because of my departure or graduation. Considering her puffy, blood shot eyes I knew it was something else.

"Mom, what is it? What is the matter?"

I walked her over to the table to sit down as she was still sniffling and blowing her nose. Grabbing my hands and holding them tight, teary eyed she looked up at me,

"You know how I took your brother into the doctor's office yesterday because he was still experiencing leg pain, well, they did a CT scan on his legs yesterday and already got the results in. They had me come into the office this afternoon and they told me your brother has cancer."

She started sobbing again. I felt like a stake had been driven right through my stomach, I felt like I might throw up and that I might pass out all at the same time. I didn't know if I was dreaming or if this was real-life. I was speechless and emotionless. I didn't know how to react; the shock had not worn off yet. Should I be sad, or mad, should I cry or get up and walk away?

I felt the tears start to well up, but I didn't want to burst out into a complete melt down in front of my mother. I wanted to be strong for her. She needed someone to lean on. She had already been through so much on her own raising two kids alone since my father had passed. I grabbed her hands and held them tight. I know it seemed cliché to say this, but I didn't know what else to say.

"Mom it's going to be okay. He is going to get through this and beat it."

I didn't know that he would beat it, but what else was I supposed say? I just sat with her, comforting her while she cried. Once she settled down she started listing off all that she had to do before tomorrow which should be the farthest thing from her mind. She rambled on how she had to let work know that she would need some time off for his appointments and treatments. A tremendous amount of guilt consumed me over leaving them here to go through this alone.

How could I leave her and my brother in their time of need? How could I even think about putting my own dreams before my brother's health and life? I felt obligated to stay and help. There was absolutely no way my mom could do this on her own with taking him to the doctor's, keeping up on the bills and the house. I felt angry, tired and upset all at the same time.

Once my mom settled in on the sofa I went upstairs to my room for the night. I had such a busy day ahead, but couldn't fall asleep. I had so much to think about and decide before the morning. Do I stay or do I leave? I tossed and turned all night, crying off and on. I tried to keep the tears from spilling over so my eyes would not be puffy tomorrow, but it was impossible to keep from crying.

It felt completely selfish of me to even feel mad or sad at the thought of not going to California with Ryan and Brooke. My brother's health and life are at stake and I'm worried about gallivanting out in California with friends. I knew what I had to do, what the right thing was to do. My mind was made up and I would stay back with my family. I rolled over to look at the clock 3:00 a.m.

Not only will my eyes be puffy from crying, but I will have dark circles to go with them. I needed to get some sleep before graduation tomorrow. I knew I needed to let Ryan and Brooke know my change of plans right away in the morning so I set my alarm for 6:30 a.m. I finally snuggled in under the blankets and immediately felt myself drifting off into a deep sleep.

My phone alarm started going off. 6:30 a.m. how can that be? I just fell asleep. As I opened my eyes I felt them stinging and knew they were bloodshot. I sat up in bed and felt extremely groggy.

This was going to be one of the longest days of my life. I got out of my warm bed and shuffled over to the dresser mirror and cringed at my reflection. I grabbed some dirty leggings off the floor and grabbed a t-shirt from my drawer, threw my hair up. I took my phone off the charger and text Ryan.

"I need to talk with you right away. I will meet you outside your house in twenty minutes."

I knew he would still be sleeping, but he will just have to deal with it. I had so much to do before the graduation ceremony run through at ten. I went downstairs to see my mother sitting at the kitchen table with her coffee. I could tell she was lost in thought just staring off out into the backyard window. She looked lonely, sad and full of worry. My heart was breaking. She finally heard my footsteps walking towards her and snapped out of her daze.

She smiled up at me and said "Good morning my little graduate."

She got up and gave me the longest hug and I just hugged her back. I had to let her know my plans to stay home and that it was not an option for me to leave.

"I'm not going to California.", I blurted out.

"Honey, what are you talking about?", she said.

"I thought about it long and hard and I'm not going to California. I'm not going to leave you here alone to deal with all of this by yourself. You are not going to give me grief about it either. I have made up my mind and I'm not looking back."

"What about college, the apartment, Ryan and Brooke?", she asked.

"None of that matters, my family comes first. I can always go to college when things blow over. Ryan and Brooke can figure California out on their own. We got this mom. We are going to kick cancer's ass!"

She pulled me close and hugged me tight again and whispered, "I love you baby girl" in my ear.

"Love you too mom. As much as I would love to stay and hug you a little longer I need to run out and talk with Ryan."

"Okay, please tell him I'm so sorry about all of this."

"Mom! No more saying sorry. I mean it, there is nothing to be sorry about."

She gave me a smile and waved her hand shooing me to get going. The morning was brisk, but the sun was shining. It felt so good to have the sun kiss my sleep deprived body as I stepped out onto the front stoup. I started the walk over to Ryan's front door and just as I was about to knock he opened the front door. Half asleep and still in his pajamas he stepped out onto the front steps and shut the door behind him.

Is there a time of the day where he doesn't look good? Delirious from sleep and sporting bed head he shot me that gorgeous smile that made me melt inside every time.

As he was yawning he said, "What's up sunshine?"

I sat down on the front step and he followed suit. For some reason, I was nervous to tell him I was not coming to California. I knew he would completely understand, but I was still fidgety and couldn't seem to look him in the eye. Finally, looking up at him with a wall of tears welling up; he realized I was upset and put his arm around me.

"What is wrong?", he asked.

As the tears spilled over I began to tell him the news of my brother. I explained how I didn't feel right leaving my mother behind to deal with all of this on her own and that I wouldn't be able to join him and Brooke in California. I kept saying over and over how sorry I was and how horrible I felt for bailing out on them.

"What are you even talking about Ashley? What are you sorry about? Your brother is sick and your family needs you. I would do the same thing if I was in your position. Don't even worry about it. Brooke and I can handle Cali.", he said as he continued to comfort me.

"I know, but I have been dreaming about this move for so long and I still can't believe it's not going to happen for me. I can't even comprehend all of this with my brother. I'm so scared Ryan, so scared that we will lose him."

"Ash it will all work out. You wait and see. Your brother is going to get better and you will be out to join us in no time."

"Yeah I hope you are right."

We just sat there on the stoup for a while in silence. He was holding me as I was resting my head on his shoulder. It felt so nice to be in his warm, comforting embrace. I didn't want to leave it. But I forced myself out and wiped the trailing tears away from my cheeks.

"I have to run over to Brooke's and tell her the news as well." I said defeated.

"Do you want me to drive you over there?", he said.

"No it's okay, the silence will be nice. I'm still processing everything and just need to be alone for a while before the chaos this afternoon."

"Okay if you are sure? I really don't mind."

"Thanks, but I will be okay. Go back to bed and rest up before today. We have a long day ahead."

He gave me the biggest hug and I turned back home and jumped in my car. I had about a ten-minute drive to Brooke's house and time to think about things. I didn't even turn the music on. Complete silence to allow my thoughts to take over. My brother's cancer was weighing on my mind, my disappointment of not being able to go to California, but most of all that I would not get the chance to tell Ryan how I felt about him.

Sick to my stomach about it all and my heart was breaking. It was like we just broke up even though we have never been together in that way. On the way to Brooke's I cried, I screamed, I was talking to myself out loud and had angry moments where I hit the steering wheel. Anybody in the lane next to me probably thought I was having some sort of psychotic break. The reality of the situation was starting to set in and I began to realize that even though I was not going to Cali with Ryan that didn't change my feelings for him or change my desire to be in an exclusive relationship with him.

I still can't stand the thought of him being with anyone else. Even though we won't be together physically I don't see why we couldn't make a long-distance relationship work until I could get out there. I could go out there for long weekend visits, we could Skype, call and text all the time. We have such a strong friendship I do not see why we couldn't make a romantic one work just as well. It's worth a shot, right? What do I have to lose at this point?

Now the question is when do I tell him how I feel? We have so much going on today with rehearsal, graduation and the senior after party at the Grove. The Grove! That's it, that will be the perfect place to tell him. That's if I can get him alone to talk.

Nothing like a last-minute profession of my affection to the love of my life. It was at that moment I realized there might be a glimmer of hope in my future. I pulled up to Brooke's house, let out a long sigh, got out of the car and walked up to her front door. After a few knocks on the door Brooke opened the door.

"Hey lady, what are you doing here so early?" she said with a concerned look.

"Can I talk to you out here?"

I started walking out into her front lawn as she followed.

"Ashley you are scaring me. What's going on? Have you been crying?"

We were now facing one another; she was touching my arm and looking at me with worry and wonder. I of course started crying as she interrogated me; I couldn't help it. I felt so sensitive right now and my emotions were not in control. I was on overload right now and just couldn't deal. I was always in control; I was never emotional and rarely ever cried. I think I was upset about being upset and crying.

I began to tell her of everything that happened and how I couldn't join her and Ryan out west. She started welling up as well and kept saying she was so sorry and how she couldn't believe this was happening the day of our senior graduation. She began to ask me a string of questions that I had not even thought about myself.

"So what is the plan? Are you going to go to community college around here? Are you going to get a job?" she said.

"To be honest I'm not sure what I'm going to do. I'm sure my brother will have a crap ton of appointments and my mom cannot afford to take off work all the time. I do not think school is an option for me right now. I mean I would love to, but doubt there will be time for any of that right now."

"You have to allow yourself to do something for you. You can't just give up everything just because your brother is sick. That sounds heartless, but take care of you too."

I know she was just trying to be nice and supportive, but I felt completely annoyed by her statement. I stepped back from her and crossed my arms and went off on a tangent. The built-up frustration and annoyance all came up and out of mouth and Brooke was the victim.

"Well for fucks sake Brooke, bring up the obvious and make me feel bad! What you don't think I don't want something for myself? I don't want to stay behind. I want to go to college, I want to have beach days, and check out guys, go dancing and drink myself into oblivion, and have late night study sessions, but that's just not in the cards for me, now is it? My mom and brother need me. I can't just leave them behind to go through this alone. What kind of person and daughter would I be if I did that? I don't need someone telling me what I need to."

I could tell she was taken back by reaction and I immediately felt guilty for the word vomit that had just spewed for my mouth. My emotions are clearly not in check. I took a deep breath and exhaled. As I looked up at Brooke I could tell she was uncomfortable and looked like she might even be scared to say another word to me for fear I might get upset again. I started to walk towards her and began to apologize,

"Brooke, I…I…. I'm so sorry. I don't know what came over me. I'm running on no sleep, I…."

She cut me off and said, "Seriously don't worry, it's fine. I get it, I get why you are upset and you have every right to be. Please don't apologize, you scream and yell whenever you need to. Seriously no matter what hour of the day it is, day or night you call me when you need to vent."

We smiled and went in for that good ol' Minnesota nice, best friend hug. I looked down at my phone for the time. It was already 8:30 a.m. and I needed to get home and shower up for the day. We said our goodbyes and went our separate ways. Now I needed to worry about getting through the rest of the day and come up with what I was going to say to Ryan.

This was my only chance and I want it to be perfect. I want to say the right things and not screw it up.

6

I decided when I showed up for graduation rehearsal that I wasn't going to sulk. The last thing I wanted was to draw attention to myself and I didn't want any pity parties. This was still a major accomplishment in my life and I wanted to make the best out of it. I had asked both Ryan and Brooke to keep things on the down low and if anyone questioned them as to why I was not going to California, just to go with the story that I had to tie up some things here before I could leave. No one needed to know more than that.

Rehearsal was to start out in the high school auditorium where we would all line up and be paired off in alphabetical order. All five hundred and fifty-two of us. It was Northfield High School's largest class yet. Next we were told to walk together with our partner to the outdoor football field where the ceremony would be taking place. Then we would file into each row until it was filled and so on and so forth.

It was the most gorgeous day a graduating class could ask for. Seventy-five degrees and sunny. We all packed into the auditorium and did as the staff directed. It felt like we were a bunch of sheep being herded off outside. I looked around at everyone's big smiles, their excitement for their futures that lay ahead, the giggles, the chatter about the big after party tonight.

I wish I was feeling the same excitement everyone else was. I wish my big after high school plans were still in my future. I felt drained and I knew what I was feeling was also showing on my face. As we were walking to the rows of chairs on the football field I felt my alphabet partner Luke Blackwell nudge me.

"Ashley, you look like hell. Are you okay? Did you start drinking already for the day?"

I decided to play dumb and realized I need to get myself in check and at least act happy and excited for today.

"What, no I haven't had a drink." I laughed nauseatingly. "Just a late night that's all."

"I sure hope you are going to perk up before the party tonight. It's going to be killer!"

I continued to laugh with him and assured him I would be up to his standards for the party tonight. As we all sat down in our chairs and continued to listen to the lecture from the principal about appropriate behaviors and rules for the ceremony. Who would think there would be rules at a graduation ceremony. Principal Durgan wanted to make it quite clear there was to be no air horns, no nakedness under our robes, no crazy dancing or acts on stage. We were to stand up, walk to stage, shake hands and grab our diplomas. No funny business.

Really!? What would they even do at this point to someone who did any of that? I'm sure I was not the only one rolling my eyes. The only plus listening to the principal lecture, hopefully for the last time, was catching some vitamin D. I took a deep breath, closed my eyes and breathed in that fresh air and enjoyed the sun kissing my face. I felt the little hairs on the back of my neck stand up and had a feeling someone was looking at me.

I opened my eyes and looked around to see Ryan peering down the row at me with a smile.

He mouthed to me "Are you doing okay?"

That smile and his question of concern gave me the butterflies. It was so great to know he genuinely cared. I nodded back to him a quick yes and smiled. Seeing him just now reminded me that

I still needed to decide what exactly I was going to say to him tonight. I couldn't do that here, but would devise a plan when I got home after rehearsal.

I needed peace and quiet to think about what I wanted to tell him. I needed a fog free head and the only way to attain that was to take a good long nap when I got home. After nearly two hours of rehearsal for graduation we were finally dismissed. I stood up and bolted the opposite way of where Ryan was standing and headed out towards the gate to get to my car. We were to report back to the auditorium in cap and gown by 5:00 pm where the ceremony would promptly follow at 6:00 pm.

I didn't feel like hanging around to gossip and chat with everyone after rehearsal. I felt like if one person asked me if I was excited for California I might burst into tears especially since I was so overly tired. I wanted to get through this day in one piece and without any drama. I felt relief once I got into my car and that I had avoided all conversations. I knew that it was only avoidable for so long because as soon as the party started after graduation that's all people would be wanting to talk about.

I couldn't get home fast enough. My bed, down comforter and pillow were calling my name. There are several hours to kill before I needed to get ready and now I didn't feel the need to rush through this day since I would not be leaving for California tomorrow. No moving checklist to worry about and whether I had everything packed, what to bring and what not. I could go home, sulk in my room, and unpack at my leisure.

As I pulled out of the parking school parking lot I rolled the windows down and turned the radio off. All I needed was silence. I needed to get my thoughts together on what I would say to Ryan tonight. Hoping he doesn't get too intoxicated tonight so he's coherent enough to comprehend what I'm telling him. It's going to be a challenge to try and pry him away from everyone and not getting interrupted.

Drunk teenagers are typically not "good drunks." They are loud, annoying and sloppy. The guys tend to get loud and dumb. Trying to one up the next classmate by doing something stupid like whipping circles in the fields, lifting "the rock" to see who can claim being the biggest brute in the class, or talking trash to their rival classmates to impress some girl. The boys would brag who slayed the bigger deer this hunting season, who caught the most crappies ice fishing, who has the louder pipes and biggest lift kit on their truck.

The trash talking usually ends up in a brawl or several brawls over the course of the night. Sounds like Hicksville to you? Well that's because it is. The drunk girls also get just as loud as the guys, giggly and annoying.

Dressing in the shortest shorts and skirts as possible, hanging all over their crushes, making other girls jealous, stumbling in the fields and laughing as they fall, trying to dance and sing along to the music blaring from someone's vehicle, groups of girls going together to take bathroom breaks which, I have never understood the bathroom trips together. What is the point in this? Do you hold each other up, help each other squat, wipe each other's asses? Dumb if you ask me. Ryan is typically the life of the party and always has girls and guys hanging around him.

I just needed to make sure I catch him on his third or fourth beer of the night and regardless of who is around take him by the hand and lead him away. This will be the last chance I have, to tell him and I'm not going to let it slip away. Not only will I have to worry about how to get him alone and what to say, but now I'm worried about how he will react. I don't expect him to stay behind by any means and I know that he wouldn't, but I just want a civilized conversation about it between the two of us.

Does any part of him feel the same? Will he be mad? Will he be happy? Or will he be speechless? Honestly I have no idea what he will feel or how he will react and that is what is making me nervous.

I might have to throw a few shots back when I get there just enough to calm my nerves, but not too much where I can't remember what I came there to tell him. I pulled into my driveway to find my mother outside mowing the lawn. As I got out of my car she stopped mowing and walked over to talk with me.

"How did your morning go honey? How did Ryan and Brooke take the news?"

I smiled at her hoping to give her some reassurance that this whole thing was not that big of a deal to me.

"Well of course they were both super bummed, but they both completely understood and said they both would have done the same if they were in my shoes. Nothing, but two supportive friends. And rehearsal was nothing short of boring."

"So glad to hear they are there for you. What are you off to do now? Do you want me to make you some lunch?"

I feel like she was babying me which I wish she wouldn't. Charlie is the one that needs to be babied not me. I get why she is acting this way. I'm sure as a mother she still feels bad and there is no way to tell her otherwise so I'm going to try to ignore it as I don't want her to feel worse than I'm sure she already does.

"Not much, I think I'm going to go crash for a while before I need to get ready for tonight. If you are okay with it, I would still like to go to the senior party afterwards and spend as much time as I can with Ryan and Brooke before they leave?"

"Absolutely, I don't care at all. What time should I expect you home?"

"I'm not really sure. If my regular curfew doesn't apply tonight could I plan to be home around 2 a.m.?"

I could see the worry-some look on her face when I threw out that time, but she quickly threw on her fake smile and said she would be fine with that since it was graduation night, but she wanted me to check in by text throughout the night. I made my way upstairs to my room and jumped right into bed. It took me all of three minutes to fall asleep. I got a solid three hours of sleep before my alarm went off to get ready for graduation. I don't even think I remember dreaming about anything.

I must have slept hard. God knows, I needed it after last night's news and the all-nighter I unintentionally pulled. I rolled out of bed feeling refreshed and jumped in the shower. I sat in the steaming water for longer than I should have. My mind was working out every scenario possible that could happen when I told Ryan my confession.

Every dialogue I ran through my head sounded awful. I was in a bit of panic about it, not knowing exactly what I was going to say. I did not want to be worked up about this and have it ruin graduation so I convinced myself that I just need to go to him unrehearsed and let it come out and play out in the moment. This concept to me was painful since I was such an organized person. Having my day planned-out was comforting to me.

But hey, life has now thrown me a major curve ball and my organized schedule and life has been thrown up in the air and scattered, so continuing with chaos seems to only fit. Might just be the new me with a new way of life. I hurriedly jumped out of the shower, blow dried my hair, put makeup on, curled my hair and threw on my dress I had picked out for this day. It was a black sundress with red floral print that I planned to wear with a mustard cardigan and black wedge heels. I'm not super fond of dresses, but thought I should spice things up on this big day.

I looked at the clock and had about fifteen minutes to spare before I needed to leave the house. I sprayed some of my favorite Paris Hilton brand perfume on. Ryan always told me he loved it and I wanted him to be able to remember me whenever he smelled that specific scent on the street. I sprinted down the stairs to see my mom was already in her outfit for tonight and my brother was playing Mario Kart on the Wii. As I came into the kitchen my mother looked at me and smiled.

"Oh baby girl you look beautiful!" Then of course as she started to cry. "I just can't believe my first born is actually graduating. Where did the time go? What I'm trying to say is I'm just so proud of you. And I know your dad would be too."

As soon as she mentioned dad I too started to tear up.

"Oh come on mom. Don't make me cry. I don't want my makeup to smear before the ceremony."

We both started laughing and then hugged. I went over and plopped on the couch next to Charlie and watched him game it up.

"Want to play?" he asked.

"No I'm good little man. I will take a rain check."

As I sat on the couch watching an intense game of Mario Kart my mind started to wondering what Ryan was doing? Was he all packed and ready to go? What was he bringing with him? Was he thinking about me and bumming that I was not going or was I not a thought at all to him? How soon would it be before he forgot about me and met another girl; a new best friend perhaps, or even worse a girlfriend?

Ugh!!!! I hate this. *Stop it Ashley*, stop feeling bad for yourself. I looked at the time on my phone and thank heavens it was time to go. I need to get out of here to clear my head from these thoughts before I go crazy.

"Alright mom, I'm off. See you guys there." I shouted walking out the door.

"See you there and good luck. Love you!"

"Love you too!" I said.

Out the door and into my car, my last time on the grounds of Northfield High School as a student. Most of the time in the summer I drive with my windows down no matter how hot or humid it is, but didn't want my curl to go away in my hair before I walked the aisle, so I settled for turning the air conditioner on. My go to station in the car was 107.9 Bob FM. Classic country radio station that played a lot of 90's country music which was my all- time favorite.

I rocked out to some old Tim McGraw and Brooks and Dunn on the way to school. These songs bring back such great memories from high school and always will. As soon as I turned onto Water Street, I started passing all the things I thought I would soon be missing; Cannon River,

Division Street and all the pretty scenery surrounding the river. It would all be in my life a little while longer. I pulled up to the parking lot of the high school which was already starting to fill up.

As I was pulling down one of the aisles I noticed Ryan just getting out of his car and pulled up to park right beside him. He waved and smiled at me as I put the car in park. He walked over to the driver's side of my car and grabbed my cap and gown as I tried to exit my car gracefully without showing anything beneath my dress. He gave me the biggest hug once I was standing and steady on my heels.

"Wow, you look great Ash! And smell great too!"

Ugh, melt! Why does he have to say things like that to me. He of course as always looks and smells great. Every time I gave him a hug or came anywhere near him I breathed him in so deep it made me light headed. It took every ounce of strength I had not to jump him and kiss him on those luscious lips.

Yikes, I'm getting carried away here. That's what he does to me and my intense attraction to him has worsened over the years. I find myself daydreaming of us kissing, cuddling on the couch, watching movies as couples do, going on date nights every month and who knows maybe down the road have some amazing sex. Yes of course I thought about that. How could I not?

"Thank you, you don't look too bad yourself." I said blushing a little.

"Are you ready to do this?" He asked.

"Of course I am. I couldn't be more ready than I am now." I said to him as we walked together towards the school's entrance.

"I still can't believe you aren't coming with to California and all this crazy cancer stuff with your brother. I am going to miss you when we leave.

"Aw, are you getting all sentimental on me?" I said teasing him.

I wanted to play Ryan's statement off like it didn't bother me and I didn't want him or anyone else to see that I was truly upset about not going, but him admitting he was going to miss me, well it felt like my insides were being ripped out.

"I'm not getting sentimental. I just want to let you know it won't be the same. Brooke and I will miss you, but will stay in touch often."

"You promise?" stopping dead in my tracks to look him in the eye.

"I promise. I swear." He said with a smile.

I felt comforted by his promise and believed he would keep it. It meant the world to me that he was making a commitment of continued friendship and communication. I felt a little at ease about the situation now knowing he wanted to stay the best of friends and wants me out there with them. We walked into the auditorium and things were crazy in there. Kids putting on their cap and gown, last minute makeup touch ups and clouds of hairspray.

The clicks of students standing doing the last of their gossiping as high school students. Brooke was already there talking with some of our co-workers from the Red Barn. She saw both Ryan and I and ran up to us and gave me the biggest hug as she was jumping up and down with excitement. Love this girl to death and she was one of my best friends as well, but this girl's choice in clothing worries me sometimes. A boho chic look.

Some of her looks are cute; she can pretty much pull off any look or style with the body she has. Other days she comes out in mismatched hippy garments and unfortunately on one of the most important nights of our lives, she was not looking her best. I by no means am a fashionista, but I know enough about it to make sure I look at the mirror before I leave the house to go anywhere public to make sure I least have matching things on.

"Oh my gosh can you believe this? We are grad-u-ATING!!!"

She said the word graduating like Kristen Wiig did on the movie Bridesmaids when she was feeling good on alcohol and volume and was talking about how she's ready to P-ARTY! She is so full of energy (all the time) and that's what I loved about her. Ryan and I both burst out laughing. As she hugged the both of us, jumping up and down with excitement I thought to myself how I'm going to miss her and her bubbly positivity. Just seeing her, her smile and hearing her giggles will brighten anyone's mood.

It won't be the same just talking with her on the phone. It will help talking, but not being within proximity of her amazing aura will take a toll on me. Ryan put his arm around the both of us as we walked over to a group of our friends to join in the chatter. Principal Durgan appeared on the auditorium stage and announced we all need to get to our seats in our assigned order, make sure cap and gown were on and gave the student body a firm reminder that there is to be no funny business or else. The "or else" he revealed earlier that day was our diplomas would be withheld.

Everyone scattered into their assigned spots. For having already practiced this one time today it still seemed very chaotic. My stomach started to flutter a bit. Not sure if it was having to be in front of a huge crowd of gawking family and friends, excitement or worry that I might trip on stage as I was known to be a tad on the clumsy side. I gave myself a little shake to get the jitters out just in time to see the procession of students had begun to make their way outside to the field. The rules were no talking while in line, no waving to someone you might know in crowd, you can smile at them and acknowledge them with your eyes, but that was the extent of it.

As we walked into the gates of the football field I noticed an array of mom's and dad's waving to get their kid's attention. Students names were being called out, flashing cameras and cell phones and yes of course there was a few students that ended up waving up at their loved ones. Although, a minor infraction, it still baffled me as to why they couldn't do as they were told. Such an issue with rules and authority. I made it to my assigned isle of chairs and started walking down the row to my seat.

Once each row was filled with students Principal Durgan walked up to the podium and announced a junior classman would be singing our National Anthem. After the anthem, we were ordered to take our seats. I glanced down the row to see Ryan and he flashed me his sweet smile. I sat back in my chair to settle in to listen to all the speeches that were to be given by staff and valedictorians. I'm sure most of the speeches were inspirational and heartwarming, but I tuned out after the first fifteen minutes of the first speech.

Only focused on what I was going to say to Ryan tonight and how he might react. To be honest I had no idea how he would react or feel. I'm trying to talk myself into being okay with whatever reaction he might have whether it is mad or excited or even if he didn't have a reaction at all and just walked away. This day was a big day for all of us and then to throw something so heavy at him like this before he left tomorrow I'm not sure how much he will appreciate it. I could not let all the what ifs cloud my mind.

I was there to complete my mission and to get my feelings out. For once I needed to think of myself and do what is right for me and not worry how it might affect someone else. I know that sounds selfish, but I don't care. I have waited so long for this. My thoughts were interrupted by my classmate next to me standing up to walk up to the podium for his diploma.

I was completely consumed by my thoughts almost the entire ceremony. Startled I quickly jumped up after him and followed the line up there. Before I knew it, my name was being called as I walked up on stage. I kept my eye on the target as to make sure I wouldn't trip by some distraction. I shook Principal Durgan's hand, smiled for a quick picture I knew my mom was waiting to take from the bleachers and walked off stage.

Working twelve years through school and that last final moment as senior lasts all of five minutes and all for a piece of paper. Crazy!!! I made my way back to my seat and painfully had to wait through another hour and a half of student names to be called. I was so antsy. I just wanted the next part of this night to begin. I wanted to be with Ryan as much as possible tonight before he left for good.

Finally, after nearly three and a half hours of waiting, Principal Durgan announced the class of 2012 to the crowd and we whipped our caps off into the air. Families and friends from the bleachers rushed down to the field to be with their graduates. Pictures were taken, hugs were given, handshakes and congratulations spread like wildfire. My mom and brother approached me with Brooke and Ryan in hand. Of course, my mother was crying tears of joy and gave me a hug ever. I just chuckled at her and finally had to start pulling away from her and said,

"Okay mom, it's okay you can let go now."

She finally did and worked on composing herself and said sniffling, "Oh sorry honey."

"Okay now before you kids run off I want to get a picture of the three of you together" she said pushing us in close.

We stood there for about two minutes straight while my mom, Brooke and Ryan's parents all snapped pictures. We all grew impatient and Ryan announced that was the end of that.

"Okay girls, you ready to get our party on and maybe a few drinks?" as he winked at us.

"Yep, I just have to turn my cap and gown in. I actually have to go get gas so I will meet you guys at the Grove."

"Ryan can I hop in with you so I don't have to worry about leaving my car somewhere?" Brooke asked.

"Yes let's go now" he said.

"See you two in a bit. I will text you when I get there."

We departed our separate ways. I hugged my mom and told her I will plan to be home around two in the morning. She of course gave me the lecture, that any good parent gives their underage kid, that although she doesn't want me drinking at all, she knows there will be beer there and that no matter what even if I have one drop of beer I must call her for a ride. I was also to tell Ryan and Brooke she would give them rides home as well. I kissed her goodbye and ran back into school to return my stuff.

I ran out to my car, as quickly as my legs would allow. I didn't want to miss anything. The flutters return in my stomach. I have been waiting for this moment for so long and I can't believe it's going to happen. I just pray I don't get so nervous that I freeze and don't forget to say all that I need to, to him.

I'm also freaking out because I need to get him alone without being interrupted and I fear this will be nearly impossible with all the drunk and annoying people around. He's always surrounded by a group of people, like bees on honey. I'm bound and determined. Even if I need to get bitchy and order people away, so be it. It's out of my character to be outspoken, but I'm beyond caring what people think.

It's my night. This is it. He will know how I feel about him.

7

Pulling into the field of parked cars near the Grove I felt myself becoming increasingly nervous and fidgety. My mind was racing as I kept going over and over the scenarios. As if I was menopausal a hot flash took over and I became dizzy. *Calm down Ashley, calm down.* I opened the windows in my car, turned up Miranda Lambert who was currently playing on my IPod, closed my eyes and took in a couple of deep breaths.

I needed to calm the heck down before I went out there. I didn't want people to see me like this which would prompt a bunch of questions and make me more nervous. I sat there in my car through about three songs, kept my eyes closed and did some deep breathing exercises. I felt myself beginning to relax more. Drinking was not part of my plan tonight as I wanted to have a clear head, but my nerves were telling me otherwise. One or two beers will do the trick to give me slight numbness to mask the nervousness, but allow me to get what I need to say out without slurring or having my head become to foggy.

Here I go. Now or never. You got this. I turned off and locked up my car. When I stepped out of the car I could hear the drunken laughter of my classmates and friends, the smell of the bonfire and the sound of Brooks and Dunn playing over the radio.

The smell and sound of a good time took away my worries for a bit. Looking at all the cars around I feel like I was the last one to arrive. I made my way into the path in the woods and walked over the wood bridge that sat over the Canyon River. It is so back here in the woods. It is one of my favorite places that we party at.

The Grove is on someone's private land that year's back some previous students found when they were four wheeling around. It's at the back of the property in the middle of nowhere. There is an old abandon house that sits on the property somewhere so I think most of us just assume the property is abandoned, knock on wood, we have never once been discovered back here. Abandoned land I'm sure is not even possible, but what else could explain the lack of life or ownership we have yet to see on the property. Once you cross the bridge you walk down the path until you reach the opening of the Grove on your left.

It's the most beautiful spot in the area besides the bridge. In the middle of the Grove is a circular field that is then surrounded by trees. It provides lots of privacy for underage partiers. Over the year's kids have made it their own. The bonfire pit is surrounded by big, long logs used as seating.

Back in the woods behind the bonfire pit there is a generator setup that is used to help power the radio and the globe lights that are strung along some of the trees. It's such an amazing spot and quite romantic if you think about it. Between the glow of the fire and the globe lights it provides perfect mood lighting. If you walk over to the opposite side of the Grove where some the field grass has not been trampled, you can lay down in the grass away from the lights and just look up at the stars or make out with whomever you are infatuated with this month. It's the perfect setting for me to tell Ryan everything. It would be even more perfect if it was just the two of us here.

When I walked into the opening of the field there wasn't a spot that was not covered. It's never been this packed before, but then again our whole senior class has never been here at one time. Before

I walked any further, I text both Brooke and Ryan, but of course I didn't receive a text back right away. I'm sure they're well off into their night of drinking and were not living on their phones like most teenagers do these days. I knew if I wanted to catch up with them I would need to make my way through the crowd. They typically hung around the bonfire area or near it so I started to push my way through to that area.

It seemed like every few feet someone was stopping me talk. Most nights I would be in the mood and want to talk with my friends, but I wanted badly to get to Ryan and Brooke and to hang with them as long as I could before the morning came. I didn't want to be rude to those talking to me so I kept my answers as short as possible and tried not to ask any open-ended questions as to avoid prolonging conversations. Surprisingly enough I was getting away with not talking California. Each person that stopped me seemed to be the same conversation and gossip.

They said things like; *oh, and did you see what she is wearing, I'm so drunk*, or who one was going to hook up with one last time. Not one conversation about if I was excited to be leaving for California. It is a relief, but I guess I'm just surprised. Sarah Giles was the eighth person to stop me and I was beginning to grow impatient as I just wanted to meet up with Ryan and Brooke. I began to fidget and look at my phone often, to hopefully give the hint that I didn't want to be talking with them.

I kept looking around in the direction of where Ryan and Brooke normally congregate, so in the immediate moment I zoned in on their location, that would be my exit cue with Sarah. She had now been chatting at me for twenty minutes and she finally brought up the subject I had been dreading all night.

"So are you excited to be leaving tomorrow for California and spending your entire summer with Ryan?"

Nervously I answered, "Well…I….um. Actually, I'm not going with them right away."

"Oh, really!? Why not?" Sarah asked looking confused.

"I have some last-minute things come up here at home that need to be taken care of before I move out there."

I didn't want her probing any more as I didn't want to go into detail about anything and get all worked up at the party. Just as she was about to ask another question I pretended my phone was ringing, told her I needed to take this call walking away and started talking on the phone like someone was really, on the other end. It seemed to work because as I turned back to look at her she had already walked away from where we were standing. Finally, I made it over to Ryan and Brooke. I broke myself into their circle and put my arm around Ryan's waist and gave him a squeeze. He looked down to see who was hugging him and smiled down at me hugging me back.

"It's about time you grace us with your presence. You ready for a beer?"

"Definitely!" I said.

He pumped the keg up that stood in the middle of the circle and started filling up my cup. He had perfected his keg pouring skills as my beer was foam free. Not sure if at our age this was a good thing or bad thing. He handed me my beer and I immediately took a long slow drink. Yikes that was smooth going down, too smooth.

I needed to make sure to milk out my drinks as long as I could because I don't want to become drunk too fast or at all. I needed to keep my mind clear, but drink just enough to calm my nerves and relax myself. Brooke came over to me and asked me what number beer I was on. I said three just to satisfy her as I knew she would give me grief if she knew this was my first and then make me chug two beers right in a row. She seemed satisfied with my answer and I finally could start my night.

It felt nice talking with my closest friends. No one brought up California, we just gossiped about the normal; who had already hooked up with who, which intoxicated kids were making fools of themselves and bets were being made if the cops would show or not to bust the party. My second beer was down the hatch and I was feeling good and loose. I was standing there thinking now was as good of a time as any to talk to Ryan. I needed to pry him away from his buddies that surrounded him and ask him to go on a walk with me.

Just as I had pumped myself up to finally do what I came to I turned around to grab Ryan's hand for a walk and I saw Miranda Stolz with a few of her friends walk up towards Ryan. I said his name to try and grab his attention before he noticed her coming and he turned around to look at me, but just as soon as he did that annoying bitch squealed his name and I lost his attention. Clearly she was already drunk for the night as she jumped into Ryan's arms and kissed him. He didn't seem to mind as I didn't see him make any attempt to fling her off him right away. My stomach dropped.

After about twenty long seconds they unlocked lips. There was no chance any time soon I would be getting him alone especially since Miranda was now around. She was giggling at whatever he was talking about and giving him playful shoves. They were smiling at each other. Then I saw it, he made a grab for her ass.

Disgusted and disappointed I filled up my cup again and walked over to the bonfire and took a seat on one of the logs sitting there staring into the fire. Pouting and wondering if I would get the chance to talk with him. It was possible to get him away from his guy friends, but it was near impossible to get him away from a pretty girl and even harder when alcohol was involved. It only made the situation worse as beer and girls elevated the hormones in him as it does any guy. He loved the attention from girls especially, girls hanging all over him in front of his buddies. It helped to build up his ego even more.

I tried so hard not to look over there at those two, but it was near impossible. She was loud and annoying and every time she giggled or screamed when he grabbed at her my head would just instantly turn. My frustration and disappointment began to build and I could feel the tears start to well up. I didn't want to cry, but I couldn't help it. The tears began to flow over and roll down my cheeks. I just kept thinking to myself your chance is over and he will never know.

Minutes turned into a half hour and then into an hour. It was now midnight and I was still sitting at the fire now alone. I glanced over to where Ryan and Miranda were standing and they were no longer there. I stood up to frantically search the crowd and I couldn't see them anywhere. Emotions began to run rapid and tears began to roll, again.

I threw my half full cup of beer into the trees and sat back down on the log. Arms crossed and all, throwing a tantrum like a two-year old. I knew what they had gone off to do and it made me so sick and well to be honest…. jealous. I only had two beers, but I began to feel nauseous and had to throw my head between my legs to keep from puking everywhere.

Why, why, why!? Why is this happening tonight of all nights? That should be me with him. We should be the one's together, off in the darkness making out and more. I swear I have the worst luck in the entire universe.

I need to calm down and get a grip. *Deep breaths, deep breaths.* The tears stopped and I felt myself begin to calm down. Not as worked up or nauseous, as just a moment ago, I still felt numb inside and all I could do to keep myself from crying again was look into the fire and try to think of absolutely nothing. A while passed and by the time I snapped out of my zombie like mood I noticed that party around me had died down.

There was no one around the fire, only a few small groups of kids left talking throughout the field. I had not even noticed people leaving around me or the night dwindling to an end. What I did notice is that I had not seen Brooke in a few hours since I first arrived and Ryan still had not reappeared from his intimate session with Miranda. Ugh! Something in me said I should start getting used to this loneliness, at least in the department of keeping men in my life.

First my dad dying, my brother's cancer diagnosis, California and now Ryan's abandonment. Still sitting by the fire, throwing myself a pity party I heard someone walking towards me as they were stepping over a mixture of beer cans and sticks. It was Ryan approaching me, hands in his pockets, walking sheepishly towards me and flashing a shy smile. My reactions were mixed. I was excited to see him coming back to me, my heart palpitations had returned as they always did when he was near me, but my head had already begun to build a wall around my heart.

His actions from tonight had bruised deeply. It was hard to put blame on him as he was technically innocent in regards to my hurt feelings. He had no idea of my intentions to profess my feelings to him, but at the same time as a friend who was leaving his best girlfriend to move to another state he should have set aside some time to hang with me on our last night together. In a guy's case his libido leads the way, over what makes the most sense. I glanced over to him as he approached me and flashed him a quick smile and returned to my stare down with the flames.

"Hey you!" he said as he sat down next to me on the log.

"Hi.", I said all sassy.

"Whoa, what crawled up your butt?" he said half-jokingly.

"What do you mean? I'm fine."

"Yeah, right."

"Did you and Miranda have a nice night together?"

"Huh? Oh, yeah Miranda. She was fine."

"That's too bad that your last sexual encounter as a high school student was just fine."

"Sexual encounter? What are you talking about Ash?"

"I saw you guys making out and then poof you guys were gone to go do who knows what else."

"Clearly you don't know me as well as you think you do. Did you happen to notice how annihilated Miranda was?"

"Yeah, so what does that have to do with anything?"

"Well since you supposedly know me so well, you should know that I do not take advantage of any of my dates or girlfriends when they are that gone."

"But I saw you two kissing and grouping at each other out there and then I just assumed when I didn't you see any more, you had gone off to.... you know."

"Geez thanks for the positive judge of my character." He said sarcastically. "Instead of jumping to conclusions like you did you should have waited to ask any of our friends we were hanging around and they would have told you that yes we were making out, as there no doubt about it Miranda is hot and when a hot girl kisses you, you don't decline, but when she almost vomited on me while we were kissing, being the gentleman that I am, I drove her home."

I instantly felt remorseful for snapping at him like I did and jumping to the conclusion he had gone off to be a man slut. This night is going all wrong. I had worked myself up tonight over something he didn't do, now he seemed irritated by me and this was not the right mood for either of us to be in when I confess. He was now standing up pacing a little bit and then turned around at me again to have another go at me.

"Since when do you care anyway who I am off with or who I'm kissing? You seem very upset about it."

"Ryan, I'm really sorry. It's just that I.... I had envisioned this night to be a lot different then it ended up being."

"How were you "envisioning" this night to go down?"

"For starters I thought with it being our last night together that the three of us would have spent the night together hanging out. But Brooke only hung around our group for maybe a half hour than I lost her. You were surrounded by your jock friends and not long after I arrived Miranda became the center of your attention."

He sat down next to me again and put his hand on my leg sending the butterflies roaring in my stomach.

"And I had plans to tell you something I have been hiding for a while now, but things just kept getting in my way tonight. I needed your undivided attention, but that has been impossible and I just got upset thinking I wouldn't be able to tell you before you left."

"You have my attention now. What is this big secret you have been hiding from me?"

When he asked me to tell him I froze. Nerves got the best of me. I just sat there staring at him, but couldn't do any more than that. Someone had ripped the vocal chords from my throat. I couldn't talk.

I had dreamt and planned of this moment forever and now here is my chance, no one around, twinkle lights surrounding me, bonfire crackling, starry night; this couldn't be a better scene to confess my feelings for him, but I'm just stuck. All I could get out was the word I and I kept stuttering through that one word and then I would freeze. He was giving me his full attention as I sat there and stuttered. He started to laugh, nudged me and said

"C'mon spit it out already. It can't be that bad whatever it is you have to say?"

He had absolutely no idea how big of a deal this was, at least to me. How I felt every time he entered a room, how I inhaled his cologne every time he walked by, how any time he touched me the butterflies swarmed my stomach and shivers were sent down my spine, how I was mentally and physically attracted to him and how it killed me every time he would have a new fling of the month or random one night stands. How right at this very moment it took all I had to not want to bring his lips to mine. This was it, this was my time. I took a deep breath and looked him in the eyes. Looked down and grabbed his hands and began to speak.

"I was going to wait to tell this when we got out to California, but now that I'm not joining you for a while I promised myself to tell you before you left. For the last few years I have become very attracted to you. This is probably weird for you to hear being we have been best friends for so long and I was not expecting this to happen either, but it just did."

His big, pearly white, smile had now gone down to a half smirk, but I kept talking as I just needed to get it out before he could say anything.

"It's not just a physical attraction to you, but I'm also in love with you."

His half smirk was now gone and I couldn't make out his reaction. Shock, might be it? Or maybe he's feeling like someone has hit him in the balls and feels sick to his stomach? He was staring at me pretty, intensely.

"I'm so sorry to spring this on you the night before you leave, but I have kept this to myself for so long now and couldn't keep it in any longer. My feelings might have had a better chance to become something more with you if I was going to California, but…"

What happened next in mid sentenced I had not expected at all. He grabbed the back of my head and pulled me in, looking into my eyes, and kissed me. I have dreamt of our first kiss for so long and now it's finally happening. It's my turn with him. Honestly, I thought he was going to be mad that I had overstepped the friend zone and developed feelings for him.

This reaction was nice and I didn't want it to stop. We kept kissing and kissing and kissing for what felt like an eternity. His full lips were so sensual against mine. The kisses were warm and a little wet. His lips, his kisses, were perfect.

My senses were going crazy; my whole body was warming up. Being a virgin and having a teenage sex drive that was now in overdrive I was wanting this to lead to more. I didn't care how much more, just more. I was enjoying being on cloud nine.

Then he abruptly stopped kissing me. His expression showed that of confusion. Not sure if his brain had now just processed what I had told him. He jumped up from the log, looking down at me still sitting there.

"Ashley, I'm sorry, but I've got to go."

Then he started to walk away. Walking turned into running.

"Wait Ryan!"

He didn't even turn around when I yelled for him. He kept running until he disappeared into the path in the woods. What just happened? We went from me talking to us kissing and now here I am again……alone. I felt broken.

Had my confession ruined our friendship? Did I scare the shit out him? He was leaving tomorrow and I would stay back.... alone. I sat there at the fire and felt the tears start to well back up and begin to spill over.

8

It was early afternoon before I woke up. As soon as my eyes opened I felt the splitting headache ping the back of my eyes. There is no way this headache came on from a hangover; I only had two or three beers last night. It had to be a stress headache mixed in with being up way too late and crying last night. Exhaustion and worry had caught up with my body which explains why I slept in until almost 1:00pm.

Laying there in my bed feeling completely worthless and not wanting to get up I realized that Brooke and Ryan were well on their way and neither of them had text me to say goodbye. I wonder what Ryan was thinking, if he thought about what I had said last night at all, did he feel the same way, did he feel anything behind that kiss like I did? Was he going to tell Brooke everything? God, I hope he doesn't say anything to her. I don't need her giving me shit because I didn't let her in on my little secret.

Also, for the fact that once she gets a hold of that information it will spread like wild fire. I wanted so badly to call him or even text him to see how he was feeling about last night's confession. I figured he would have called me if he wanted to talk about it. I just need to let fate take its' course. That is if there is any fate to be had for our future together.

Instead of making it weird between us I decided it's best to try and move forward and act like nothing had happened. I sat up in bed and grabbed my phone off the charger. After starting a text to just Ryan I added Brooke to the message as I didn't want to make him feel uncomfortable.

Hey guys sorry I was not up this morning to see you off.... late night. Hope you have a safe flight to Cali and things go smoothly when you get there. Wishing I was there with you. Love ya guys. –Ash

Immediately after I sent it I felt something in my stomach. Not butterflies, but nerves. I didn't know if Ryan would respond and if he did what would he say back? Is he mad, sad or confused? Gah! I hate not knowing how he is feeling about last night or what he thinks about it all. This obsessive analyzing is going to drive me right over the edge.

About a minute later after I sent the text Brooke replied, "Just landed and on our way. Miss you already lady!"

"I'm so jealous! Have fun and send me lots of pics and Snaps!!"

"We will. Let's Face time tonight."

"Looking forward to it! Don't forget about me here in Minnesota."

"Ha ha. You will be here before you know it with us. TTYL!"

I hope Brooke is right. I want to be there SO very, badly starting the next chapter of my life as well. That sounds so selfish considering what my brother is currently dealing with. It feels terrible to be throwing myself a pity party knowing what he will be enduring and how hard my mother will be working while taking care of her sick child. In my mind, there was no other option than to stay with them until he gets through this sickness.

I refuse to think he won't get through this. My head needs to be on straight. I need to get my mind off Ryan and California and what better way to do that then working my butt off to help mom pay the bills, taking my brother to his appointments and helping around the house. Why has he not text me back though. I mean honestly can't he at least fake it that what happened last night isn't messing with his brain.

He's playing the guy game; "if I ignore her it will all go away." He can't play that game with me. I'm his best friend. As a friend, he owes it to me to acknowledge my existence. Clearly that is not his train of thought.

Wow, I really, must have messed with his mind, throwing that confession at him. At least I know for a fact that he has not said anything to Brooke as she would have called me immediately about it after her flight. A relief for now. Throwing my phone down on the bed and sitting there staring into oblivion thinking of what to do to be productive. As crappy and tired as I'm feeling today, not sure I will be moving any faster than a snail's pace.

My one and only goal for the day was to go talk with Mr. Simon to see if he had room to hire me back on for the summer schedule. The Red Barn was only a seasonal joint, opening late spring through early fall. I needed to work as much as possible not only to help mom with the bills, but build my savings for when I do move out to Cali. I have high hopes that I don't need to look for more work beyond fall because I'm confident my brother will be better by then and I will be living in California before Thanksgiving. I dig out some of my packed clothes from the boxes sitting on my floor.

I don't even bother to brush my hair or my teeth. I trot down the stairs and meet eyes with my mother.

"Hey there sleepy head! Glad you could join us for the last half of the day" my mom said giggling to herself.

She is always laughing at her so-called jokes or lines. She thinks all of them are funny even though some are not and are outdated. It's cute though. At least she has some sense of humor.

"Good morning. I mean good afternoon. Sorry I slept the day away. I didn't expect to be out so late."

"Don't apologize. You are only young once. Certainly, you deserved to have yourself a good time with friends after working so hard in school."

"Sorry to get up and run, but I'm going to run over and talk with Mr. Simon about putting me on the summer schedule. I want to try and catch him soon before he puts out the next schedule."

"Oh honey, I'm so sorry that you have to work your summer away. I feel terrible your plans have been put on hold. Are you absolutely, positive this is what you want to do? I really think I can manage if you want to go."

Of course, this is not what I want to do, but what I must do. It's the right thing to do. Family is forever and we need to stick together.

"Mom, seriously it's not that big of a deal. What's a few more months at home with my two-favorite people? I do not mind at all and I want to be here for Charlie as he's going through all of this."

Tears start to well up in her eyes as she makes her way around the counter to give me a hug. I start to laugh at her. She smiles because she knows I think she's overly emotional about stuff.

"Oh stop making fun of your mother and give me a hug." We hug it out once again.

"Really, mom I have got to go. I need to catch Mr. Simon before he leaves for the day."

"Okay, okay. Get going then."

Grabbing a banana for the road and run out to my car. I make the all too familiar drive to the Red Barn. During my car ride I keep glancing down at my phone to see if I got a text from Ryan. Each time I glance down it only brings on disappointment. As I pull in the parking lot I see Mr. Simon's car is still there.

Hustling out of my car to catch him before anyone else shows up for their evening shifts. I walk in and catch him off guard.

"Hey there little lady, what in Sam hill are you doing here? Aren't you supposed to be long gone to California?"

"Yes I was, but I decided last night I was going to miss this place too much and so I stayed behind."

He chuckled. "Nice try, what are you really doing here?"

The details started to divulge from my mouth once again. After he was up to date on what was going on with Charlie, I begged for my job back and requested as many hours as I could get through the summer. He didn't hesitate for one second and gave me my old job back. He said he was happy to have a seasoned employee back, as good help is hard to find these days.

9

I took a few days off before starting back to work to get boxes unpacked and my room back in order. It was such a relief to know that one thing was going right and I had a job lined up for the summer. During this time, I also went to one of Charlie's appointments. Unfortunately, this was not an appointment filled with good news. It was glum and depressing.

Charlie's oncologist laid out the plan of action with my mother and Charlie. Dr. Goodall did not believe in sugar coating things for his pediatric patients. He didn't want them being surprised and believed there is always better outcomes and reactions from his patient's when they know exactly what is going on with their care. Since his type of cancer was an aggressive one, they wanted to hit it hard right away. Chemotherapy and surgery to remove the tumor was in the forecast over the next few months.

I felt so bad for my Charlie boy. It didn't look like he would be enjoying his summer like the rest of his friends. It would be filled with doctors, hospitals, fatigue and sickness. It was all so surreal that something like this was happening to someone I knew, let alone my little brother. He looked so sad sitting in the chair listening to all of this.

I decided I was going to be strong for him and for my mom. There was no time for weakness, at least not for me. I nudged him and stuck my tongue out and got him to smile. That smile right there is going to get us through this.

It had been almost two whole weeks, since Ryan and Brooke left for California and still no text or calls from Ryan. I couldn't figure out why he was ignoring me. Guys don't hold grudges for so long. When you piss them off or say something wrong they usually get over it than less than 24 hours and then it went back to as if nothing ever happened. Ryan cutting off communication with me was making this way worse.

I would take him talking to me about hot bikini babes in California over the silent treatment. I know he has been busy getting the apartment together and job searching as I was getting those updates from Brooke, but you can't honestly tell me he doesn't have even two minutes to send a quick text? Brooke was also still in the dark about it all, as she has not mentioned one word about it. I'm going to give him through the weekend and if I don't hear from him I'm going to call. Sunday morning came and still no word from Ryan.

I called Brooke for our weekly chat.

"Hey! What are you and Ryan up to today?"

"Ha! Tending to our hangovers. Last night was brutal."

"Yuck that sucks. What did the two of you do last night?"

"The neighbors invited us to a beach party at Huntington Beach. They thought it would be a nice way for us to meet some more people. It would have been nice to meet other people, but instead I buddied up with Mr. Jack Daniels and by 2 am forgot all of my friend's names that I just met."

"Oh no Brooke, that's terrible. How did Ryan make out last night?" I asked pryingly.

"Ryan made out with someone?!" she asked confused.

"No Brooke, I don't know that. I'm asking if you knew how his night went? If he met a lot of guys and girls there?"

"Gotcha. I don't know. We went our own ways when we got there. I saw him a few times throughout the night talking to different people. It's all so hazy right now. Ask him for the details" she said groggily.

"Ugh Ash I'm sorry, but I need to stop talking. The room is spinning as we speak."

I had to know if Ryan was around so I could catch him.

"Wait! Did Ryan come home with you last night? I mean I just want to know if he's around so I can try and catch him at a good time."

"We Ubered home together, just the two of us. I can't imagine he is feeling any better than me though. You might have better luck catching him this afternoon."

"Okay feel better ya goon."

She mumbled a good bye and hung up. What a relief to know he hadn't brought anyone home or gone home with someone else. It's still hard not to be jealous regardless of his feelings towards me. These feeling were not going to go away overnight. They have been there for so long and have built up so much.

I knew it was going to take time. But damn, the thought of him going home with other girls was tearing me apart and I knew it was only a matter of time before that happened especially once they started establishing themselves more out there. Why did I have to fall in love with him? The last man I loved this much, my dad, left me too and left me broken hearted. That whole thing was beyond anyone's control, but it took me year's to finally be at peace with why he left us.

Ryan was the next consistent man in my life next to my father. I have loved Ryan longer than I ever did my father; do to the fact that Ryan has just been around longer. My father's death left me confused, angry and sad. Looking back, I grieved that loss for a long time. When Ryan came into my life I was leery of him and stand offish. Don't get me wrong, I was excited to have met a friend, but I was guarding my heart at the same time.

I realize now the leeriness was probably because I observed we were becoming great friends and the thought of him leaving me or ending our friendship scared me. I constantly obsessed that Ryan and his family would move away and he would be gone. I always mentally prepared myself to get that news one day from him. Although, we have been friends for so long and our friendship has always been solid my jealousy streak always spiked when he had a new girlfriend in his life. I'm not sure that it's actual jealousy or leaning more towards the side of fear.

Fear that I will be ignored and forgotten during any of his relationships. I didn't want to be his rebound friend when one of those ended. I wanted to be number one in his life always. Expecting that of him sounded crazy and I knew it was a lot to ask so I never asked that of him. Being the great human being he has always been to me I was never put on the back burner until his junior year with Katie. We still hung out and talked, but not nearly as much pre-relationship.

With my history of losing my father and having a hard time letting other male figures into my life I knew that if Ryan and I didn't get to some normalcy back that I was going to fall fast and hard into the deep abyss of grieving. Grieving the loss of another great man that provided stability in my life and friendship. All because I decided to grow intimate and loving feelings for him.

Damn it Ashley, why?!

We must reconnect. I'm willing to play graduation night off as not a big deal, act like the confession never happened and pretend it's not bothering me that he does not feel the same way as I do about him. I can overcome my feelings for him, but I will not and would not make it through the loss of our friendship. I need him in my life. I pick up my cell and dial Ryan's number. As it starts ringing I'm begging out loud to myself for him to pick up the phone.

"C'mon, c'mon, please pick up the phone." It rings about five more times before his voicemail picks up.

"Hey Ryan! It's me your best friend, Ashley Monroe. I would love to hear from you and see how things are going out there. In all the years, we have known each other we, have ever gone this long without talking? It's kind of weird. I hope you are doing well out there and I can't wait to hear from you. Call me when you get a chance."

I hung up disappointed as ever, hoping he was sleeping and didn't hear his phone ringing versus the scenario where he was awake, saw my name come across his phone and ignored my call. The rest of my day was spent constantly staring at my phone, hoping he would call me back or at least text me back. Does he think ignoring me completely is going to make me go away? Does he think I will give our friendship up this easily? If he does, then he has another thing coming.

I understand that what I said and the actions that took place after I talked have now made him feel uncomfortable, but was he just going to give up on our eight-year friendship because of a minor hiccup? I swear guys are worse than girls when it comes to feelings. Immaturity had to be playing a big part in this. I'm not going to let an excuse like immaturity, not emotionally developed and stupidity ruin us. By dinner time I had still not heard a word back from Ryan.

Instead of calling him I decided to reach out (again) via text.

"Hey are you alive out there? Can't seem to get a hold of you and wanted to see how things are going for you in the big city? TTYS!"

I stared, yet again, at my text to him in hopes I would get an immediate response or at least the confirmation it had been read, but none of the above occurred. I'm not giving up! Two hours later, still no response, I decided to take to Snap Chat. I was going to try every avenue I could think of to get a hold of him, but also without drawing the attention of others like Brooke. Social media of any sort was out of the question.

Posting on any of those avenues would only draw in unwanted attention and drama from others that can't help, but stick their noses in others business. I swear about half the town spends three quarters of their day scanning the feeds for new juice to expose. They thrive on other's drama. That's all this situation with Ryan needs right now is to be all over Northfield. It would only make things worse.

I started my Snap video to Ryan.

"Hey stranger! I have been trying to get a hold of you for a while now and I'm starting to get a little concerned that you might be injured, lying in a ditch somewhere. Kidding! But no really, just missing my best friend and wanted to make sure you are doing okay on your own. Maybe we can have a catchup coffee sesh via Facetime or something? Let me know. Peace out!!"

I tried to keep it light and funny. I didn't bring up anything that should upset him or make him uncomfortable, only that as a friend I missed him and wanted to catch up. Minutes passed and he still had not checked the snap. I cannot keep doing this, driving myself crazy checking for new texts, phone calls and Snaps. What to do to keep myself busy?

It was a perfect night for a walk so my mom and I went and power walked our way through the neighborhood. Thankfully, I didn't have to do much of the talking on the walk as I was distracted with checking my phone. I should have left this darn thing at home. She talked about how the next few weeks were going to be rough on Charlie with the start of his chemotherapy. She kept reiterating to me what the doctors already had said to the both of us; that Charlie would have good and bad days.

He would be fatigued, more than likely he would get sick, he would be in pain, he would be weak. I didn't want to talk about this, it made me sick to my stomach thinking of my brother in such a vulnerable, fragile state.

"Mom do you think we can talk about something else?"

"Oh, yeah, sure. Sorry, it's just that I want you to be mentally prepared for this and know what to expect" she said.

"I know, sorry. I am prepared. The doctor explained it pretty thoroughly at the last appointment."

"So glad you could be there for that too. It's always nice to have two sets of ears in case there is something I don't remember in regards to his treatments and care. I'm so forgetful, more now than ever."

Normally, when someone is talking to me I make it appoint to make eye contact to show my engagement in the conversation as it's a pet peeve of mine when you are trying to have a chat with someone and they are constantly texting, Instagramming, or surfing the feeds and not showing two bits of interest in what I'm saying. There are times when this happens that I want to pull a Ron Swanson, from *Parks and Recreation*, by grabbing their cell phone, pulling out a hammer and smashing their phone. I'm almost positive this would be frowned upon and they would lock me up in the St. Peter asylum. It's my generations' debility and I swear it will one day lead to the downfall of all human connection. My dear mother was trying to get some normal human interaction and here I was, every three minutes, pulling my phone out from my pocket, opening all apps that I had tried communicating to Ryan through and checking them to see if there was any response back from him.

I felt terrible doing that to her, but I couldn't help myself.

"No worries at all. I just don't want to think about all the negative to come with his upcoming treatments and want to focus on thinking and talking positively about his treatments and how we can look forward to doing normal things when he is feeling 100%."

"See that's my girl. I knew I could count on you to be our positive support system", she said as she gave me a one-armed hug.

"Have you talked to Brooke and Ryan lately? How are they adapting out there?"

I didn't want to tell her who specifically I have (or lack there-of) have not talked to, so I broadly told her,

"They are doing awesome out there. They have gone out with a few of their neighbors, met new people and now, sounds like they are both on the hunt for a job."

That answer seemed to suffice her inquiry into my California peeps new lives. Relieved that there were no specific questions about Ryan that I would have to conjure up a fake answer to, considering I knew nothing new about him or any details about his new life out there. Ugh! I checked my phone again...nothing. When we got back to the house I continued distracting myself with playing ball in the backyard with Charlie, finishing up our three-month long puzzle, shower and catching up with my Netflix shows. Midnight rolled around, what a surprise, nothing from Ryan.

I needed to sleep and stop obsessing. Before falling asleep I promised myself and our friendship that I would do my due diligence to get in at least one conversation with Ryan by continuing once a week to call, text, Snap, Facetime and email him. By the hand of Zeus (out comes my dramatic side) I will get through to him.

10

True to my promise, I text, snapped, called, emailed, message in a bottle (okay that one is an exaggeration) and Facetimed the crap out of Ryan. Not a single response, ever. Almost weekly I was in contact with Brooke and got bits and pieces about Ryan from her. I tried hard not to ask too many questions about him, not wanting her to suspect that Ryan and I had not actually talked since graduation night. Unsure if Brooke is just that much of an airhead (bless her heart) or if she's just that preoccupied with her own life there, that she has not caught on to anything yet.

There is a part of me that wishes she knew about the situation because it sure would be nice to vent to a girlfriend. Beyond Ryan and Brooke, I did not have any real close friends. I would call them more of acquaintances. I had no one close to home that I could confide to. Everyone around me was busy with summer activities, jobs and shipping off to their first year of college.

I couldn't put all the blame on others as I, myself, was busy putting in as many hours as possible at the Red Barn, my brother's appointments and helping-out around the house. After a few weeks' out in California, Brooke found herself a full-time waitressing job and a part time job as a yoga instructor. She said it didn't take long for her and Ryan to realize just how expensive it was to live out there. Granted they had they had funding from Ryan's parents to last them a while, they knew that wouldn't last forever. She also mentioned that her and Ryan barely saw each other, do to their work schedules.

Every now and then they would have some afternoon's off together, but when they were not working they spent their time sleeping, drinking, sunbathing and doing yoga at the beach for Brooke and auditions for Ryan. Brooke mentioned Ryan had landed himself a job as a waiter and that he was going to a lot of auditions for acting jobs as well. Ryan has absolutely no experience acting or modeling, not that I thought he needed any professional experience. Ryan had natural talent at anything he does in life. With his confidence, ambition, good looks and natural talent it will only be a matter of time before I see him on TV or the big screen. That's one way I will get to see him.

Listening to Brooke and just how busy socially and professionally they were out there, it pinged me with a smidge of jealousy. I was busy here at home, but not the kind of busy I dreamed of being in this stage of my life. My life was currently consumed with pizza, meds, puke buckets, needles, tears, doctors and cancer. I'm trying to stay positive and keep my head up through all of this, but I do have my moments where I cry myself to sleep at night. To bring some light and hope in my life I have been living vicariously through Brooke via social media pictures and our talks.

If I can't physically be in California I will dream of it and be there through her. Her Insta stories, pictures and snaps were filled with her wonderful smile, goofiness and good humor. In my life where there is currently doom and gloom she has been filling it with light, whether she knew she was doing that or not.

Charlie boy was in his sixth week of chemotherapy and unfortunately things were not going well. He was weak from the therapy and very sick. There have been a lot of sleepless nights at home for all three of us. My mom and I would take turns every few days waking up with him when he needed someone. He has been sick from the chemotherapy, which is a common side effect but, we have been lucky with him that he has not caught anything else that would land him in overnight stays at the hospital since he has a weakened immune system from chemo.

Since Charlie started chemo we have all been very vigilant with washing our hands, sanitizing and taking our work clothes off before entering the house as to prevent exposing him to any bugs lurking on our clothing that we might have picked up when either of us was out and about. We had to cut back how much Charlie went out in the public to minimize his exposure to germs. Obviously, this was not always possible, but we managed. Instead of outings to restaurants, movies and Target we substituted them with walks, low traffic beaches and dinners in backyard and summer baseball games sitting dang near the right, outfield line. It was better than him sitting indoors and feeling sorry for himself. We do as much as we can to keep him busy when he is feeling up to it as to keep his mind off the things his body is going through.

When he was not in pain or throwing up he was in great spirits considering the circumstances. I was so proud of him and impressed by his braveness and courage. If I were in his shoes I'm not sure I could hold it together as well as he has been. He also did not have to worry about losing his hair because two days before started chemotherapy he decided to shave his head. Week nine of therapy arrived and with it came a fever and hospitalization.

Any time a cancer patient gets a fever 100.4° degrees or over they need to be seen immediately in the ER for evaluation. Fevers in anyone can mean their body is sick and fighting off infection and usually can be dealt with at home. In a cancer patient's case their bodies must work twice as hard to fight a simple infection off and if not dealt with appropriately and effectively can quickly become dangerous for them. Charlie had been fighting this fever for a little over 24 hours and when Tylenol could not bring it down we had to take him in. We all three went into the ER and were scared as this was our first time dealing with a cancer related ER visit.

We had no idea what to expect or what this visit would bring. When we called his oncologist to let him know the situation he did want us to come to the ER, but requested we enter through the back door as he did not want Charlie sitting in the germ-infested waiting room. Once we arrived to the ER's back door they quickly gave Charlie a mask and ushered us into a quarantined room. Vitals were taken, blood samples were drawn and a chest x-ray to rule out pneumonia or any other complications. His blood tests revealed his white blood cell count was lower than a normal cancer patients should be, but with every protocol they followed and test they completed they could not locate the source of his infection.

The fever continued to spike and it was decided he needed to be admitted until his fever came down. We knew this was always a possibility, but it didn't make it any less scary. Once he was settled in his room and the nurses left him alone for a bit I sat down next to him on his bed and held his hand. My mom had left the room to find us some snacks and drinks. After a few minutes of sitting next to him in silence he began to cry.

"Hey, hey what's this all about little man?"

"I'm scared Ash", he sobbed as the big alligator tears rolled down his red, sweaty cheeks.

"I've tried so hard all day to not cry around mom. I don't want her worrying even more then she is already, but I can't help it anymore."

"Buddy, it's okay. You are going through and have been going through so much. It's only normal for you or anyone in your condition to cry. As far as mom goes, crying or not crying mom is going to worry no matter what you do or say. That's just what mother's do." I said in a reassuring voice.

I was trying so hard myself not to cry in front of him. I wanted to stay as calm as possible. The unknown of all of this was so scary and stressful.

"I just feel so terrible. I want this to be over, I want to go back living a normal life, playing with my friends and playing sports.", he said sniffling.

"It's hard, I can't imagine how you are feeling, but I just know you are going to get through this. Maybe not as fast as you would like, but soon. I just know it. Let's get you through whatever infection is going on now, breathe and take this all day by day. For now, let's see what's on the tube."

We laid there in each other's company watching our favorite movie *The Avenger's.* It must have been what he needed because five minutes into the movie he stopped crying and calmed down. That was hard to see him like that. I can only pray and hope this is the one and only hiccup he has. He has been so fortunate up until this point.

Both my mom and I stayed the night with Charlie in the hospital. The staff informed us he was only supposed to have one overnight guest, but they would make an exception for tonight since this was his first admission. My mom slept in a reclining chair next to Charlie's bed and I slept on sofa that was also in the room. A restful nights' sleep did not actually occur, between the nurses coming in every thirty minutes to check his vitals and the moaning and groaning of Charlie in agony. What we thought was only going to be a one to two-night stay ended up being a five night stay.

Test after test, scan after scan was run and not one single doctor could pinpoint the source of infection. All parties were frustrated by this, because without a conclusive answer they couldn't give him any specific medication that they knew for sure, would take care of the infection. Broad-spectrum antibiotics were all that he could currently be on and we had to pray hard that would do the trick. This admission also set him back in his chemotherapy treatment as he couldn't receive while he was sick from infection as it would only weaken his immune system more. This stay was hard on all of us obviously, Charlie experiencing the worst of it.

My mom and I rotated staying overnights with him to try and prevent the both of us being tired and worn out at the same time. Regardless if you got to sleep at home the night before it seemed we were both always tired and were starting to resemble zombies. Sitting up at the hospital day and night just sucks the energy right out of you for some reason. I swear there was an energy scanner at the nurse's station that required you to deposit ten percent of your energy each time you passed. For a healthy human, being in a hospital was draining; I can't imagine being Charlie and starting off sick coming into this. Poor guy!

You can list the cons and negatives of having a hospital admission all day long, but with this stay there was some light. From all the scans Charlie, had they could see that his tumor was shrinking, which was great news. Shrinkage meant the chemotherapy was working and he was one step closer to getting the tumor removed. Hospital admission had set him back in his therapy by one full week so he still had four more weeks of therapy before they could officially schedule the surgery. Although, the tumor was smaller they needed it to shrink as far as it would go with twelve weeks of therapy, as to lessen the complications of removal during surgery and make recovery smoother.

He was headed in the right direction of beating this thing with only a small bump in the road. By day five his fever was down to 99.0° degrees. If it stayed down and continued down over the next day they thought, he would be discharged by tomorrow afternoon. Charlie's appearance and demeanor had made a 360 over the past twenty-four hours. He was gaining some color back in his cheeks, the all-over body aches and pains had subsided for the moment and his appetite was returning. It was so good to have him back to normal (or as normal as a cancer patient can be.)

Insistent, my mother stayed with Charlie the last night. I stayed until about four o'clock that afternoon and then left to go home to shower and sleep. Over the past week Brooke had tried calling and texting me as I had missed our Sunday morning phone call as I was in the hospital. I felt bad I had not responded to her at all, but I didn't have the energy to explain to her what was all going on. All my energy and attention was focused on my family.

After dinner and a hot shower, I would call her back to catch her up on Charlie. Trying to unwind and relax I turned the bathroom into a steam shower. I went to my favorite playlist on my phone that I compiled for days like this to help me relax. My relaxation playlist included a mixture of different artists and genres of music; blues, country music oldies, but goodies, Coldplay, and Leon Bridges. Music heals and calms and I couldn't do without it.

As I was showering I had a billion things running through my mind. A million and one to do lists. Then as I was thinking about my upcoming call with Brooke I realized this was the first week in a while I had not bombarded Ryan with my calls, texts and messages. Heck, I do not even think I thought of him once this whole week. I was so consumed with everything going on with Charlie.

Had Ryan even thought about me when or wondered what was wrong when he didn't hear from me this week? Was he concerned at all about me? He knows about Charlie's cancer, was there no cause for concern in his mind? He has not once even reached out to at least check on Charlie. They were like brothers when Ryan was home. How dare he let what is going on between us (whatever Ryan thought that was) get in the way of his and Charlie's relationship.

What kind of friend is he to me at this point? I could feel myself getting worked up which was the opposite of what I was going for. I grabbed my bath robe from the hook next to the shower and jumped quickly out of the shower. Dripping hair and all I needed to call Brooke and see what it is that Ryan had been up to. Granted Ryan did not know currently just how sick Charlie was so I felt like I needed to give him the benefit of the doubt that he still did care about it.

I dialed Brooke. “Good gracious woman! Did you fall off the face of the Earth or what?” she answered without even saying hi. I chuckled at her.

“Sorry girl, I have been really consumed with the family at home. I kept meaning to get back to you, but time just got away from me.”

“Is everything okay at home? Is Charlie okay?” she asked concerned.

“Charlie has actually been really sick this past week and was required to stay for a few nights at the hospital.”

“Oh my gosh, is he okay? How is he doing now? How are you holding up?” she rambled off all at once.

“He is doing a lot better now. The first days were rough and we were not sure what was going on. Doctor’s said he had an infection and because his body is weak from chemotherapy it took him longer to fight it off. He is doing better now and should be home tomorrow.”

“Ashley, I’m so sorry you and the family are going through this. You should have called me.”

“I really wanted to, but we are not really supposed to be on our phones in his room and when I’m not up at the hospital, I’m sleeping at home. It’s all so exhausting. Sorry.”

“Don’t apologize to me. I understand why you couldn’t call. I feel bad I can’t physically be there for you.”

“It’s all good. Talking and venting does me just as good as if you were here. Enough about Charlie. I need to talk about other things. What’s new with you?” I said anxiously.

“Um, not too much. I’m so busy working both jobs I do not have time for much else other than the beach. Ryan and I don’t see each other anymore either. He's upped his audition game. To be honest I'm not sure if he even sleeps anymore."

"That's good for Ryan. He's seems to be doing what he set out to do when he moved there and I'm happy for him. Happy for the both of you" I said as enthusiastically as I could.

"To be honest I'm not really sure what I came out here to do. You and Ryan had these big plans to come out here and at the time it sounded fantastic. BUT now that I'm out here, it's beautiful and all, but man it's hard work trying to live the life of an adult. Adulthood is hard!"

We both sat in silence after she said this and five seconds later burst out laughing.

"Welcome to real-life Brooke. I have come to learn life beyond high school is not all unicorns and rainbows either. Are you planning to come home for Thanksgiving or Christmas this year?"

"Doubt it. Unless my parent's fly me home I can't afford to fly home. Plus, it's hard to ask off work during the holiday season. You will be living out here by then, anyway right? Was that not your plan?"

"That was and still is my plan, but I will just have to see how things go with Charlie. I need to make sure he's healthy before I move. My mom can't do this without me."

"Bummer! I was looking forward to having you out here. I know it's out of your control and I swear I'm not trying to make you feel bad, but I'm still a little bummed."

"Nothing is concrete. There is still a chance I will be out there before Thanksgiving. We just must wait and see. I should get to bed now. It's been a long day. Tell Ryan I said hi."

"Will do, get some rest and tell your mom and Charlie I said hi and I'm thinking of the both of them."

"I will and thank you. Good-night!"

11

I was up at the hospital by noon the next day. Charlie had a great night and was fever free. His night nurse had informed my mom before she ended her shift that the rounding doctor said he would be discharged home today, but they needed to make their rounds put in the official orders of discharge before he could leave. Charlie was bouncing off the walls, he was so happy he was going home. He was dressed and ready and the doctor has not even been in yet to check him over one last time.

The nurse could not give us a specific time when the doctor would be in as we were not his only patient to be seen this morning. We still could have a few hours here before we leave. Charlie was sitting on his bed playing his Nintendo DS while my mom and I played a round of war. Two hours passed and Charlie was becoming impatient. He was now on a fifteen- minute schedule of asking "Can we go yet?"

It was like being on a road trip with a five-year old asking "Are we there yet?" every few minutes. Normally, I have patience with Charlie, but on day six, locked in the confines of a hospital room, again, my patience had begun to wear thin.

"Chill out Charlie!", I snapped.

"Geez, someone is cranky." He said with a sly smirk

"I'm not cranky. I want to get out of here just like you do, but asking if we can go every minute of every hour is not going to make things go any faster. You heard the nurse just as well as we did that the doctor is making his rounds. Chill out and stop bugging, mom."

"Someone needs a nap", he said teasingly.

"You know kids, I'm not even going to scold you for nagging at each other or for Charlie bugging me. It's sweet music to my ears considering the situation we were in a week ago", she said to us with a smile.

Charlie and I looked at each other after she said this smiled. Thankfully, fifteen minutes later the rounding doctor and Charlie's oncologist walked in. The nurse took one last set of vitals, the doctors looked him over and began dictating their notes into their portable computers that logged them. We were given strict orders to keep an eye on his temperature over the next few days and bring him back in should he get another fever, he was not to go out in public anywhere for the next few weeks as they needed him to get through the chemotherapy without complication.

As the doctor's and nurse where finishing up with Charlie, I felt my butt buzz. I pulled my cell phone out of my back pocket to see a text from Ryan. RYAN! Oh, my gosh, it was RYAN! After months of no communication from his whatsoever he texted me back.

I had to do a triple take at my screen and shake my head a few times to make sure I was really, seeing this. All I could see were the first two words of the text "Hey, I heard…." I opened my home screen and went into my text messages. I went into Ryan's text. My heart was palpitating. I started to read it,

"Hey, I heard Charlie was in the hospital. Sounds like he is doing better. Tell him I said to hang in there. Take care."

I'm relieved that he does still care about Charlie don't get me wrong, but I'm beginning to feel a little selfish and jealous after reading that text. After all this time, not one word in that text was geared towards me or how I was doing or feeling. Really!? Not even how is big sister holding up. At least his text about Charlie was a start.

I relayed the message from Ryan to Charlie. He immediately lit up as he was grabbing his stuff on his way out the door of his hospital room. I hadn't even realized the doctor's left the room. We were officially on our way out of this joint. I wanted to reply to Ryan's text, but decided to wait until we got home so I could make sure I had all the time in the world to continue texting with him back and forth all night.

To play it safe when I texted him back, I was not going to bring up graduation night or even hint at it. Clearly from the past few month's history of lack of communication on Ryan's part graduation night was a sore spot. I would only stick to subjects like Charlie, his life out in California, his job, auditions and what not. It was the safest bet. Moving past that night and working through it and my feelings internally is the only way I can think of to get him back. I was willing to sacrifice my feelings for our friendship.

When we arrived home, my mom told me Charlie begged the entire car ride home for her to let him go outside for a bit to play or take him to Target to get some new DS games. It's like what the doctors said directly to his face went in one ear and out the other or they were speaking a foreign language to him because none of it registered in his little brain. But, who's to blame the kid. He has been on lock down for so long. As hard as it had to have been for my mom to say no to him she stuck to her guns and the doctor's orders and told him no.

When we arrived home I helped mom get Charlie settled on the couch for the time being. Even though he did nothing, but lay around at the hospital he had doctor's orders for continued rest at home for at least the next three days. They needed him to build him strength back up before starting chemo again. Charlie moped for a while on the couch and once he realized there was no use in crying and complaining he resorted to playing on his iPad. Mom was in the kitchen starting on an early dinner and that was my cue to go to my bedroom to text Ryan back.

The dust flew off the butterfly's wings that had laid dormant in my insides for the past few weeks. I was feeling giddy and hopeful that Ryan and I would soon be back to the way things were between us as friends. We needed to get back to that otherwise, when I move out there this fall it would make the situation extremely awkward. I started my response back to him;

"Hey friend! I'm so happy to hear from you! Charlie is finally back home as of an hour ago. It was a rough week, but the warrior that he is, he pulled through. How are things out there going for you? I can't wait to hear all about it."

I didn't want to seem too anxious and request to call him so I left it at that, implying that there should be plans to talk about him. Expecting an immediate response back from him I frowned when three minutes had passed and he had still not even read the text. Figuring it had been almost two hours since he originally texted me so he probably got busy doing other things. I would give it some time. Wiped out from it all and too excited to leave my phone's side I turned on my laptop to binge watch some Netflix shows.

I wanted to be readily available to text him right back once he responded. Startling myself awake from an unintended nap; I was breathing heavily like I had just finished a mile run. Six o'clock! Crap!

I can't believe I fell asleep. I knew I was tired, but not so tired that I drifted off without even realizing it until two hours later. There must be at least a dozen texts back from him, I'm sure of it. Quickly grabbing my phone from my night stand and glancing at the locked screen for text alerts.

Wait, what?! There's nothing, no new texts, no missed calls. What the hell is going on? There must be something. Maybe my phone is on the fritz or something.

I unlocked my phone and went into my text messaging app to see if there were new one's waiting and it was just a glitch of my phone that didn't send the alert through. Nothing! Not even one damn text back. I went into my last text I sent to him to see if he had at least read my response back.

Nope, still not read. Delivered, but not read. Unbelievable! What kind of sick joke was this? Why would he text me the one time and not even have the decency to give one little text back, even if it was only a few words?

Honestly, I'm surprised. How could he be this mad at me? What can I do or say to make up for this?

Crushed. This is the only word that explains how I'm feeling at this current moment. Crushed because he didn't respond, crushed because I felt that I knew deep down he didn't want our friendship any more, crushed because I no longer knew what to do to save us, crushed because another important man in my life is abandoning me. I didn't want to tell Brooke and have her vouch for me, that was something you did in middle school when you sent a girlfriend to do your dirty work because you were to shy or embarrassed to talk to your crush yourself. I didn't want to involve others, as it would only cause drama.

I'm not ready to give up my best friend for the mistake I made in loving him. How is loving someone a mistake? I understand that love doesn't always go both ways and that is either party's right to feel that way, but how do you go from being best friends for eight years to nothing. It's like Ryan and Ashley never were. The demise of us was complete.

I'm out of ideas at this point. Flying out there on a whim right now is not optional with things so crazy at home. Not knowing what to do at this point or how to handle this I needed to get it out there to him that I'm willing to move on and forget about my deeper feelings. I want to promise him I would move on and go back to the way things were. But, we need to be on talking terms before I move out there.

This was not the route I wanted to take with him. These were not the things I want to bring up or say to him, but since my woman's intuition is telling me to, this will be my last plea to him; it's what needs to be done. Opening my last text with Ryan I began to write.

"Hey Ryan, I'm not sure what is going on between us right now? We haven't talked since graduation night, which is weird considering before you left we would talk multiple times a day. I have been putting forth the effort to get a hold of you, but it's lacking back on your side. I appreciate your recent text to me with concern over Charlie. You text me about Charlie and then when I responded back to you, there has yet to be a return message from you. Assuming this all must do with the conversation that was had on graduation night. Yes, the topic that arose from that conversation and the feelings revealed where way out of left field. To put that on you before you left for California was not fair to you. I do not know what I was expecting by revealing this to you. I panicked knowing I was not going to California with you, but I didn't want you to leave not knowing how I was feeling about you. I do not expect you to feel the same way, BUT I do expect you to continuing being my best friend. I'm willing to work on moving past those intimate feelings for you, but you also need to realize it will take time for those feelings to subside. To be honest that is already happening as I have been a little put off by your behavior and lack of effort to keep our friendship alive. I need us to get past this awkward post-confession kiss phase and get back to the old Ashley and Ryan; friends. Best friends at that. Let me know if this is something you can move past before I move out there with the two of you?"

After hitting send I took a deep breath. Feeling relieved after saying all of that to him. Yet again, here I was letting him know how I was feeling. I have never been one to be so emotional or talk about my feelings with anyone. Normally, I hole up feelings and emotions inside and every few months when it all got to be too much, I would have a night cry before bed.

Or whatever was bothering me would go away after a few days. That was something I self-taught myself to do because I always instilled in myself and believed I had to be strong for my mom and brother. I couldn't put the burden of emotions and weakness especially on my mom considering she has been through so much since the loss of my father. So here I am, second big emotional spill and

I do not believe this one will benefit me with a positive outcome.

12

It's been about five years now since Ryan's last correspondence to me. The last time I had any contact with him was the day Charlie came home from the hospital from his first admission when he was fighting his cancer. That was the day I knew friends Ryan and Ashley were over. I sent him my last message that night begging him to forget my confession, pretend it never happened and return to normalcy, but he proved to me to have no interest in any of that. After my last text to him that night I never heard from him again. No calls, no texts, no comments on social media, no snapchats or emails. Poof! We were done.

For a little over a year I struggled with this loss. I literally experienced the same feelings and emotions as I did when I grieved the loss of my father. It was terrible, especially since I went through it alone. To this day I still have never told anyone about my graduation night confession. Every time my mom, Brooke or anyone else brought up Ryan I would make up excuses as to why we had not been talking.

Eventually, everyone stopped asking me about him and I could stop sweating about what lie to make up next. Since the abandonment of my best friend I put up barriers around my heart. Good luck to anyone that tries to break through. Not going to happen. It's not that I didn't want to be in a relationship and find love, but last time I tried that is scared me shitless and broke me too badly.

Over the past four years I have had a handful of semi-serious relationships. None of them lasting longer than seven months. Between those I would say I have had about a baker's dozen of one night stands not including what I have going on with Jake. So, I'm not completely dusty when it comes to dating and my sex life. Unfortunately, my problem with dating besides the worry of getting hurt is I always compared my short-lived boyfriends to Ryan. Bless their hearts they didn't even know they didn't stand a chance.

I swore up and down I wouldn't do the comparison thing, I tried and tried again not to, but without fail I always did. It didn't matter how nice they were, good looking or well-mannered they were never good enough. The thick as steel wall, electrical and barbed wire fence, land mined filled ground and twenty cloned Hulk's (Avenger's fan coming out again) that guarded my heart made it damn near impossible to penetrate. About three weeks after my final text to Ryan I knew I had been defeated and he was not returning to me let alone talking to me in anyway. To keep myself as distracted as humanly possible, I plunged myself deep into work when I was not helping taking care of Charlie.

Charlie got through his next four weeks of chemotherapy without incident. His tumor shrank down enough that they could perform surgery to remove all of it. After surgery, the tumor was tested to see how serious and how far along the cancer was. Unfortunately, like I said before his type of cancer was an aggressive form of pediatric cancer and had a high risk of relapse. When the biopsies of his tumor came back it was serious enough that they felt he needed twenty-four additional weeks of chemotherapy.

Twenty-four weeks if he didn't get sick and require hospitalization which with cancer patient's is not likely. With the new treatment plan that meant that I would not be moving out to California before Thanksgiving and so, I did not. Brooke, of course, was upset that I was not moving out there any time soon, but she understood why. I can only assume she told Ryan that news at the time, but I'm sure there was relief on his end with this news, as this gave him the distance he clearly wanted. He no longer needed to worry about me nagging him when I got there (which I wouldn't have nagged him anyway), he no longer needed to worry about the awkwardness, or moving out of the apartment completely if that's as far as he was willing to go to avoid me.

My mom insisted that I keep my plans to move out there, but she was down-right crazy if she thought I was leaving her here with Charlie to try and do it all on her own. If I would have been that selfish and left her I know my mother would have figured things out, but she has done so since I was little, but I did not want to intentionally inflict that stress and loneliness on her. Twenty-four weeks spanned into thirty-two weeks as there was delays in having continuous therapy do to a few more infections and hospital admissions. Some admissions where a quick few days and others were drawn out into a week. Each time just as scary as the last.

Some stays were calm, some were agony, some we knew we were going home the next day and some stays we didn't know if Charlie would be leaving the hospital bed ever. Their little bodies get so weak from the chemotherapy and the cancer itself and so when they get an infection or other sickness it scares the shit right out of you. You do not know sometimes if they will ever be coming back home with you. It breaks you over and over again to hear them cry out in agony that, "it hurts, it hurts." So many ups and downs with cancer.

So much unknown, so much waiting and praying and hoping. Happy to report that those days are over for us. A little over a year after Charlie was diagnosed with Ewing Sarcoma, June 10th to be exact, we received the best news of any of our lives. Charlie was NED (No Evidence of Disease)! Charlie, out of all of us was the most elated. He was able to join his baseball team again that year, go camping with his friends, run around the neighborhood with his neighborhood friends and what he was most excited about was that that following school year he would have a normal schedule of school.

No more weeks at a time of missing school because he was sick or couldn't be exposed. He was a normal kid again and loving it. We were all loving it. After Charlie was free of disease all of us got back into a normal routine. Charlie went back to school and doing his extracurricular activities, mom went back to work, she also formed a local support group for other parents in the community and surrounding communities that are dealing with or have dealt with having a child with cancer or other debilitating or terminal diseases.

With any cancer, there can be a chance of relapse. Every six months up to two years of being disease free Charlie had to go in for scans. This was a normal and precautionary follow-up plan for cancer patients to help ensure and confirm they were still living with no evidence of disease. Every two weeks leading up to his scan mom would start to become anxious and worried about what they might find. Charlie on the other hand was busy making up for the year he lost being a kid.

He did confide in me one time that he did get nervous and scared until he heard the scan results were NED, but tried to keep a smile on because he didn't want mom to worry more than she already was. Two years of no evidence of disease his scans went to once a year and he still to this days is without disease and leading a normal, healthy childhood. After that first year of Charlie being back to normal I decided not to move out to California. Part of me was scared to deal with Ryan face to face and the baggage that whole situation would more than likely bring. Brooke, was now traveling around with an acroyoga group and was rarely home.

She quit her waitressing job when she landed this acro gig and was on cloud nine with her new life and boyfriend, Tom. When she was back in Los Angeles she told me she typically stays at Tom's place. She begged me many times to still move out there and said I would fit in great and make a life for myself there in no time. California and the people I knew out there no longer were what I thought it was going to be. Brooke was still my friend, but from phone conversations to pictures and videos on social media feeds she seemed like a different person then I grew up with.

Not the Minnesota girl I once knew. Ryan and Brooke had made themselves a new life out there without me and I was a little bit bitter about it all, so I decided to stay back in Minnesota permanently. I do not regret staying back to take care of my brother and mom, but I would be lying if I said I wasn't a little bit jealous of what Ryan and Brooke had out there. Once my mind was made up that I was never leaving Northfield, I plunged myself into working. My plans of being a nurse I put on the back burner.

I wanted to save money so that I could pay for college as that would help lessen the burden of student loans. Having my own place was in the works too. It's not that I didn't love living with my mom and Charlie, but it was just time for me to have my own space and independence. For the next two and a half years I picked up almost a full-time schedule at The Red Barn. I had Thursdays off which allowed me to run errands and hang out with mom and Charlie. Since the barn was only open seasonally I also picked up a nanny job for a local family. Personally, I was not super fond of being a nanny, but it paid the bills.

After eight months of working my butt off I had saved enough money to rent a little apartment off Division Street in Northfield. Independence was an amazing feeling. I could stay out as late as I wanted, eat and drink what I wanted, dust or not dust. I loved my new-found freedom. I'm still in my little apartment and still loving it just as much as the day I moved in.

I continued to work at The Red Barn and my nanny job until I turned twenty-one. That moment I turned twenty-one I wanted to change something in my life. Since graduating high school I hadn't done anything exciting or daring. I hadn't taken any chances in life. No cliff diving, no tattoos or piercings, no whim purchases like motorcycle. I…. was…. LAME!!

I was still not ready to jump into nursing school and I was okay with that. I didn't want to rush into anything so confining like nursing school. It was a huge commitment time wise and financial. I liked my little (lame) life. It was going great.

My 21st birthday my mom had to work a double shift at the hospital so I took it upon myself to go out drinking. Since I didn't want to drink and drive I walked across to the bar kiddie corner from my apartment, The Contented Cow Pub. I had been dying to check it out since I moved in to my apartment. Every summer, from my window, I could listen to the bands and musicians that played in their outdoor courtyard by the river. That bar was always so lively and now, I could legally join in the fun.

I remember throwing on some makeup, my best pair of jeans, a dressier black tank, threw in some beach curls and walked over for my first legal beer. When I walked up to order my drink I had no idea what to get. It was all craft and imported beers. Looking at the alcohol percentages next to each beer I was a little worried. I didn't want to be full board intoxicated and not be able to enjoy my birthday.

I drank off and on with my mom every now and then, so I knew I was going to be a light weight. Looking up at their drink board with a deer in the headlights look that's when I met the owner and my boss Greg.

"What can I get you little lady?", he said with a grin.

"Yikes, I'm not sure? Give me the lightest beer you have please."

"What's the occasion? Are you meeting some friends here for drinks?"

"No." I felt dumb saying I was alone on my 21st birthday.

"It's my 21st birthday today and I came over for my first legal drink. I live in an apartment kiddie corner from here. Most of my close girlfriends are out of town and my mom is working tonight, but I could not, not come out for a drink on my birthday"

"Well, no shit! Happy birthday! This one is on the house." I chuckled at his response.

"Thank you! That is so sweet. Are you sure?"

"Of course. Minnesota nice, right?"

"Right!" I said.

"Also you are not going to sit alone on your birthday and drink by yourself at least not in my bar. Nancy come tend the bar while I have a drink with this nice young lady!"

I didn't have the heart to tell him no and to be honest, I was happy to have the company on my birthday. Greg, was a short, round, middle aged man with salt-n-pepper colored hair who smelled stale popcorn and spilled beer. He also reminded me of Elvis as his thick, sideburns replicated Elvis's to a T. Greg sat with me on the patio that day and we chatted away for hours. Every time we laughed over something that was said I giggled to myself because of his belly jiggling every time he laughed.

We talked for hours that day like we were old war buddies that hadn't see each other in ions. Never imagining I would spend my 21st birthday like that, now looking back I wouldn't have wanted to spend it in any other way. That very same night is when Greg offered me a job at the pub. He told me our three-hour long conversation was the best interview he had yet (Obviously, I had no idea I was interviewing for a job). Wanting change in my life at the time I jumped at the opportunity.

It was the best birthday present I got that day. The next day I put in my two week notice at both The Red Barn and with the family I nanny. Never did I imagine I would be a bartender. I have been working there now for a little over a year and still loving it! If I would have followed society's life schedule, I would have been graduated nursing school last year and working in some area of healthcare. My life's plan has gone everywhere, but on track.

As a little girl, I dreamed of my dad walking me down the aisle at my wedding, but he died; I was supposed to go to nursing school in California right after high school, but my brother got sick. Instead of college I worked two jobs after high school to help my mom pay the bills while my brother was fighting through cancer. I unintentionally lost a best friend in life; I started a full-time bartending job instead of going to school. Am I bitter about my life not going as planned? Maybe while in those very moments, but never did I dwell on that feeling of bitterness. Life works out for those who make the best of how things work out.

13

My shift tonight at the bar was insanely busy, from start to finish; restocking beer for tonight's shift and preparing the bar for all the craziness that a live band brings to a bar in a college town. The Northern Light's band always attracted double the crowd, then on a normal Friday night. The band has such amazing talent and not to mention easy on the eyes. I had heard them play for the first time at Rippy's bar in Nashville last February and was blown away. Our group stayed there and listened to their entire set. I think half of their tips made that night came from us.

They are a laid back and fun group of musicians. After their set, they came around and chatted with the crowd. That's when I met one of the main guys, Jake. We hit it off and made each other laugh and swapped contact info. Strictly on a friend basis, well, it was "friend only" status in the beginning.

We ended with the olé' "If you are ever in town, reach out." Which was a strong possibility considering his buddy in the band, Nick was from Minnesota as well. Once I got back to work that Monday I had somehow convinced my boss at The Contented Cow Pub to hire them to come up to Minnesota to play at our bar. They have now been coming to play for us about every two months and each time, I swear, there are the regulars that come out every time, plus a hundred (or more) new fans. It's getting to the point where we are going to have to start turning down patrons coming in because when Northern Lights is here, we are near max capacity.

It's too bad, but our little bar in the alley cannot hold their growing fan base. When I say, I work in a bar in an alley, I do not mean in the big city in a slimy, trash filled alley. It's the cutest, little riverside bar in Northfield; located on the bottom level of a building that once was the original Northfield City Hall and then converted to a fire station. When the owners bought the building the bottom level where the bar is today it was half developed and half rock and dirt.

It's amazing to see what it is today. In the spring and summer months we host bands outdoors by our deck and patio area which allows more customers to attend their concert. They are kind of a big deal around here now. I should also mention that once (okay maybe a few times) I have had some one niters with Jake. That was never my intention when I asked Greg, my boss, to bring the band here, but we make each other laugh, have a good time when we are together and things just happen. His sexy voice might have a little to do with it too.

We have never been anything more than friends (with benefits) because of the long- distance thing which is fine with the both of us, as neither of us is looking for anything serious. We have a great time when he is in town. We hang out like normal friends do; baseball games, drinks, apps and then usually back to my apartment for the night. The hooking up is extremely hot and sexy. We are both attractive, young adults who have common interests, and like to have some fun, sweaty, romp sessions with no strings attached.

Jake is about 6' feet tall, slender but, toned, dazzling green eyes, grown out sandy blonde hair (not long like down to his shoulders, but not clean cut). Born and raised in Tennessee he has a country boy way about him. Adorably handsome! Yum!

Before my rendezvous with Jake began, I did date and hook up off and on throughout the years. Even between meeting up with Jake, I hooked up once in a blue moon with an attractive college boy that flirts with me during my shift. Dating or hooking up with the patrons is not ideal, but there are no rules about at the pub and it's not habitual so I do not worry about what others might think. Things stay fresh in the bed between us, I believe because it's a once every two-month booty call, that stretches over a period of two to three days when he is in town. The long periods between allow us to learn new things for the bedroom (not that I sleep around often at all) which keeps it interesting and exciting.

It's really, laid back which I like. It works for the both of us, so until either of us gets into a serious relationship with another or his band hits the big time we will keep on what we got going on. Normally, the band was playing here about every two months, but things are really, starting to take off for them in Nashville and I haven't seen him in about six months. Needless, to say, I am more excited than normal to see him and catch up (wink, wink).

As I was wiping down the bar and stuffing napkin holders I heard a breaking news report from TMZ on the TV. Usually, I do not fall into watching or listening to this show, but the subject of their breaking news report was Ryan. Seems the lime light Ryan was seeking out is now fading to black. It had nearly been four years since I heard from Ryan. Yes, my best friend (ex-best friend) Ryan Black had decided our friendship meant nothing to him and moved on to what I guess he considered bigger, better and more important things in life.

As I grow I make new life goals or plans. Currently, my life goal is to live a simple, happy and humble life. That's the path I'm on now and I have no qualms about it. From the sounds of it on TV, Ryan should think about adopting a simpler way of life. He might not be in the predicament he has got himself into out there.

14

Over the last three months, on a weekly basis Ryan was all over the entertainment news channels, tabloids and social media. He got himself into a whole heap of trouble. On a Thursday night, he was pulled over as someone called him in because his car was seen swerving all over the road. Not only was he issued a DWI, but they also found a few bottles of prescription drugs that were, not his, on the front passenger seat which landed him in a court ordered ninety- day rehab program.

Off and on throughout the years I had read or heard that Ryan was quite the partier out in LA. He was always at the biggest parties being thrown, seen with the prettiest of women and was well known as being a "good time", (insert eye roll emoji). Whatever that meant. Never did I imagine he would get into drugs. Alcohol I figured because he was already a heavy drinker our senior year of high school, but never did I think he would fall into the peer pressure of drugs.

Ryan Black did end up making a name for himself out in Hollywood and was now the hot shot movie star he always dreamed of being. His name and face was everywhere. Good thing for me I didn't watch a lot of TV, I avoided watching any of his movies and never "liked" or "followed" any of his social media pages. In the grocery store, Target or gas stations I would see his face on the cover of one of the entertainment magazines and just chuckled at it as I walked by. Never once did I purchase one that he was on.

The history between Ryan and I was long logged away in a book collecting dust on a dark damp shelf in a library somewhere. It took me a ridiculously long time to move on, so long that I'm not going to say just how long. Avoiding anything "Ryan" is just the easiest way for me to forget him. It is impossible to completely forget him, but not supporting his career by not buying a movie ticket or a magazine or giving him that so called "like" helped and was justifiable by me. It's what works.

As cold and black hearted as this may sound I do not feel bad for him, not one bit. Ryan is a grown man who can make his own decisions. He knows the difference between right and wrong. One night, he decided to gamble and lost. Fact: I'm glad he got caught before he ended up hurting someone on his alcohol and drug influenced escapades.

Two people I do feel bad for are his parents. They still live right next to my mom and I have seen them a few times in town throughout the years. Two weeks after Ryan was admitted into rehab and his name and face was still being plastered all over the media, they came into the bar. They looked tired and stressed and came here to relax their nerves with some good craft beers and nachos. Knowing how a small-town works, they were more than likely being thrown scowls, stares and pointing fingers.

Ryan, I'm sure never thought about how his actions would affect his family back home. If he did care his actions proved otherwise. The Blacks were not seated in my section, but as I was on my way to one of my tables I stopped by for a quick hello. Their faces seem to light up when they saw me.

"Ashley! How wonderful to see you!" Mrs. Black said enthusiastically.

Mrs. B was a petite woman, short stature, but slender, almost black hair like Ryan's that fell just below her shoulders. This woman was always so full of life and cheerful, but I could tell the years and more than likely recent events with her son were wearing on her. She looks tired. Poor girl.

"You guys out for a big night on the town?" I said.

I wanted to avoid talking about our common interest as I did not want them to feel obligated to talk about him or his situation. Plus, it was best to be avoided as there are prying ears everywhere.

"Ha, ha, we are too old for nights like that anymore." Mr. Black chimed in.

Not to sound weird, but I could see where Ryan got his looks from. Both of his parents were good looking people, but Ryan gained a lot of his build from his 6'4" father. He was still a toned man for his age, dark brown hair and always wore a five o'clock shadow. I do not think I ever saw Mr. B clean shaved. He looked just as worn as Mrs. Black.

I felt terrible for them. They were not them old selves.

"Too old!? I do not think so. You are never too old for a good time."

"You are too sweet Ashley. You are looking great and happy. Happy we ran into you here."

"Thanks Mrs. B. It was great to see the both of you too. I suppose I should get this order over to my thirsty patrons. Have a great night!" I said walking away.

Victory! No mention of Ryan, what a relief. I do feel bad, I want to be there for the Black's, but it's too hard for me to walk down that road again. I have worked too hard to keep him off my mind. Damn, you Ryan for hurting your own parents.

Never pinned him as the type to drag down others. For his sake and his parents' sake I hope he makes it through rehab successfully and can continue forward with a clean and happy life.

15

News of Ryan and his shocking prescription drug addiction had finally begun to die down. Thank God! After months of his face being plastered all over the television and social media I had become more annoyed than anything at the media's persistence to invade his personnel life more than they normally do. As bitter as I was towards him, I was still annoyed for him by all this extra, negative attention he was receiving. Let the man get better in peace instead of trying to dig up more dirt on him.

News shows and media can be so cruel and relentless. For the most part I didn't feel bad for him, but I had my moments of weakness that quickly subsided. Ninety days of rehab for Ryan had now come and gone. Surprisingly, no one seemed to know his current whereabouts after he completed rehab.

Did he fall off the band wagon already? Did he leave the country? Did he enter the priesthood? Not likely. Even the media did not know his whereabouts.

His social media accounts have been hushed since he entered rehab. Complete silence from Ryan Black. He was good at disappearing and not talking to people he didn't want to. I know this from experience.

Northern Lights was in town a whole month earlier and they were playing tonight so the bar was bustling for preparations for the night's crowds. The crowds tonight were expected to be larger than normal because this past week was college finals, so students were out celebrating before they went home for the summer. Warm weather itself would draw in people from around town. Who doesn't love to sit on a patio drinking after the longest five months of winter Minnesota had ever experienced? The Contented Cow had obtained a special permit and permission from surrounding businesses to let the crowds spread out onto their properties if needed. All staff was on deck, which was a first in the history since the bar had opened.

Greg, the owner and even his wife Jill were on hand. We didn't want to sink our ship before it even sailed. Jake had stopped in that afternoon to say hi before the rest of the band arrived for setup. Looking as good as ever in his baseball cap, white t-shirt and jeans. I literally just described the stereotypical look of a musician.

It was not stereotyping, as that's the way almost all the musician's I knew dressed. Northern Lights are more in the country music genre, so instead of sneakers and black combat boots they almost always wore their cowboy boots. Gets a girl all riled up thinking about it. We smiled at each other as he walked over for a hug.

"Looking good Jake, new boots?"

"What? No, same ones I wear every other time you see me."

"Oh, huh. Well, maybe you should get a new pair. Switch it up a bit, maybe snake skin? You never know might attract more attention from the ladies in the crowd with some sexy new snake skin boots."

"I'm not looking to attract the attention of anyone tonight, but yours. I will walk over to your place after our set is done. I have something new to show you." He said winking.

"Oh, eh, I don't think tonight is going to work", I said feeling really, bad.

"Oh, really!? Do you have other plans tonight? A date or something?"

I could tell he was disappointed. I wanted more than anything to hang out with him and indulge in his amazing body, but I knew I wouldn't get out of here until way past closing time. By then nothing but sleeping would be on my mind.

"No, it's not that at all. It's just that I won't get out of here until way past closing time and I have already been here since one this afternoon. As much as I want to see anything new that you have to offer, I guarantee my body and eyes will be limp by the time I stroll back to my apartment."

"You know that I can change that in a heartbeat. It won't take much to wake up your senses once I get started."

"Gah, stop taunting me. Really, more than anything I want to, but I just know me. I can't tonight, but I swear I will make it up to you tomorrow night. We can spend the day hanging out and doing whatever we want once I wake up for the day."

He looked like a sad puppy dog after I denied him again.

"Ya, no I get it. I will come up to the bar during breaks on set tonight. If I don't get a chance to talk with you tonight before we head out just text me when you get up tomorrow."

"Okay Jake, thanks for understanding. I should keep at it though before we start getting busy. Break a leg tonight!"

I hugged him goodbye and got back to stocking glasses behind the bar.

By 3:30pm almost all the patio tables were full and a steady swarm of people just kept coming. Northern Lights was not even set to play until 7:00pm and seeing how busy it was already I knew this was going to be a long, crazy and interesting night. At least once the band came on I would have some decent music to listen to, to help pass the time. I was scheduled to be behind the bar tonight which personally, I loved this spot the most. You still received tips, but didn't have to fight your way through the air tight, drunken crowds where you ended up spilling half the tray of beers often because some drunken asshole was not paying attention.

Another reason I was thankful to be working indoors tonight was to be out of the smoke. Minnesota adopted a statewide ban on smoking inside bars, restaurants, bowling allies, etc. in 2007. Thank heavens! Obviously bartending and waitressing to smokers' outdoors was not as bad as if they were smoking inside, but when you get body after body stacked on top of one another like a herd of sheep it feels no different. You still smell and feel like you were stuck inside a chimney for hours. Tonight, would be one of those nights.... sheep night!

My night was well under way; I had never seen the place so busy especially once the band started. It was a great night for live music, it's warm but, breezy. I was running around so much behind the bar I could feel the upper lip sweat start to build up. Ugh gross, I hate when I get all sweaty. Showering will be a must before I jump into bed, I will be way too sticky and sweaty to bypass a scrub down.

Tank top and shorts were a good call for tonight. My voice would be almost non-existent by the end of the night because of all the screaming I'm doing just to get their drink orders people. There was barely time to relax and enjoy the music. I wouldn't even be able to tell you a single song they have played on set. My mind was sorting orders; Oatmeal Stout, Sweet Child of Vine,

Belgian White and El Chavo and couldn't process much more than that. Not even lyrics to the classics they were playing outside that I knew by heart.

There was not even time to pee. Not sure I would even make it through the herds of sheep. That's exactly how I described it and that's exactly what it looked like. Everyone around me was starting to sway, on their way to feeling good or on their way to vomiting because they were beyond feeling good, they were numb. Eyes where heavy, one eye closed and one eye opened, slurring speech, "I love you man's", and extra hugs from intoxicated ladies on the prowl.

Playing the part of sober bartender, it was entertaining to watch and annoying at the same time. God, I hope I didn't look half as annoying as some of these girls do when I'm drunk. How embarrassing! The crowd inside seemed to be making its way out to the patio. Perfect timing because I needed to restock some supplies, clean glasses and wipe things down.

It was a nice little break from the screaming, booze infused people yelling at me for more drinks. Trying to translate their slurred speech was getting to be impossible. Was there such a thing as a Rosetta Stone-primary language-intoxication? I bet I could get a whole pitcher of beer just off the counter. I grabbed a rag and started wiping down the bar counter.

Finally, I could hear the band and they were playing one of my favorites, "Tulsa Time" by Don Williams. Getting into my work and singing along I happened to glance up for a quick second over at the booth kiddie corner from the bar. There was a younger man sitting there in the shadowy corner just staring at me. I didn't think too much about it as it was not something out of the ordinary and went back to wiping. As I did the hairs on the back of my neck started to stand up and I got a chill down my spine.

Something was telling me to look up again. Curious to what my instincts were telling me I looked up to that darkly lit booth. Our eyes met, he smiled and discreetly waved. Frozen, blankly staring in disbelief and in mid wipe. He stopped waving at me after about a minute of me standing there not reacting.

My mind, heart and body didn't know how to react. Those first two minutes I just stood there, heart pounding so loud it drowned out the music and barely breathing. A small flutter in my stomach flickered only for a millisecond and was quickly crushed as the anger rose threw my entire being like a tsunami. Ryan.

He had the audacity to show up here at my work. He was home. What is going on? What my eyes where currently seeing, my brain was trying to process. The anger seemed to awake me from my frozen state.

It took me a minute to process whether I was drunk, dreaming or experiencing real-life. Pinch. Nope, real-life. I convinced my body to start moving and walked around from behind the bar, briskly past the booth he was sitting in while staring him down. I made it out to the deck railing and stood there, racing heart and all, waiting for Ryan to catch up with me.

For the five seconds, I stood there alone with a billion and one thoughts and questions racing through my head. Why was he here? What did he want? How dare he show his face after all these years. Did he think we are still friends? Is it okay to punch someone while you are on the clock?

Ryan caught up to me on the deck and stood right beside me. Fuming, it took me a while to turn away from the band and face him once he started talking. Time has agreed with Ryan, he was still the tall, dark and handsome guy I grew up with. As much as I hate to say it, growing old agrees with him. If possible, he was a little better looking than when I last saw.

A little more on the rugged side with his five o'clock shadow and more toned than when he left. The stress of his most recent scandal didn't seem to age him one bit.

"Hey Ash, how have you been? You look great!" He said cheerfully with that bright, white, perfect smile.

His hands were stuffed in his front pockets and he seemed relaxed. Gah, he looked good standing there. Stop it Ashley! Remember what he put you through. He said it like we were long lost friends, meeting up to happily talk about our lives, loves and lust, as if nothing ever happened.

"How have I been? Really!?" I said sternly, but in a low tone.

Still on the clock I didn't want to draw attention to myself since I was not behind the bar where I was supposed to be. Gathering by his choice of seating back in the bar in the low-lit corner of the booth, he didn't want people to notice him either.

"After five years of radio silence on an eight-year friendship, that you my friend gave up on, you think I just want to willingly pick up on a happy note, as if nothing ever happened?"

That perfect smile soon diminished off his, still melt me your gorgeous, face. The hostility in my voice, crossed arms and frowning brows must have surprised him. Did he think I would rush up to hug him welcoming him back? Welcoming him back into my life is the last thing that is going to happen. Too much hurt, too much time and energy has been spent on this man and I can't waste any more.

"Eh, I, eh, um" stuttering through what he was going to say next.

"Ashley, I'm sorry for being a dick of a friend to you. You didn't deserve the stone silence from me. I handled that situation in the worst way possible."

As he said this he tried grabbing on to my arm as if to comfort me, but I quickly backed away.

"Save your apologies. I do not want anything to do with them or you."

"C'mon Ashley, don't be like this. Don't push me away. I miss my best friend."

"Best friend!? Best friends don't ignore you, best friends are there for you through the toughest of times and best of times, best friends talk, laugh, and visit together no matter the distance, no matter their status, no matter what they have going on in their life. Best friends we are not as you have done none of that for me since you left that night."

"I know, I know! I was and am a shitty person and I'm trying to work through it and get better. Please I really want to make it up to you."

"No, sorry I can't. It's too hard. There is too much history I do not want to dig up again. You abandoned me when I needed you the most."

Tears were starting to well up in my eyes. Looking at him, being near him, pleading to me I could feel my wall start to crack. I didn't want him to see that he was getting to me. How could I weaken so fast? It's not fair.

I built this defense up to prevent weaknesses like him to enter. How in the hell is there a fault in my wall? I needed to get away from him. I started to walk away and he gently grabbed my hand.

"Please Ashley, I need you." He said begging.

I could tell by the look on his face he was feeling desperate, he was alone, he was weak too. Serves him right. I stared back at him still holding his hand not knowing what to say. I do not want to give in to him. His looks and charm aren't always going to work.

I can't let him break me. As I stood there staring back at him I felt a tear roll down my cheek. I quickly pulled my hand back and walked away leaving him there. Panicked I rushed to find Greg in the crowd. I apologized to him telling him I needed to leave right away.

"What? Why? Is everything okay!?" He asked concerned.

"Yes, I'm just having some sharp stomach pains and need to leave. I can't be exposing everyone when I feel like this."

"You go on ahead and rest. Someone will cover the bar."

"Thanks Greg. I owe you one. I will text you tomorrow."

I ran full board from the patio area back to my apartment. Frantically struggling with my key, I finally got my door open only to slam it shut and then locking myself in. I stood with my back against my door, huffing and puffing from my short run back. Dazed and confused as my emotions started to flood my body. Alone in my apartment I said out loud to no one, but myself; *Please Ryan, leave me alone.*

16

Last night when I got home I turned off my phone, smoked a little weed to help me relax, showered and went to bed. I do not smoke weed on a daily basis. I use it when I'm feeling anxious and I'm only anxious when my mind starts to wander towards Ryan. The past two years that has not been often, but I always keep some on hand should the need for it arise. When I turned on my phone that morning it dinged five times.

It could not be from Ryan because he didn't have my new cell phone number. I had changed it a few years ago when I switched cell service carriers. Two were from my mom seeing what I was up to for the weekend and if I planned to stop by. Then one was Greg checking in to see how I was feeling. The next one, from Jake asking where I disappeared to last night and if I wanted to meet up today for lunch.

The last one from a number that was not stored in my phone. The text read; "Can we please talk? Let me explain myself. Please."

Clearly that one was from Ryan. How did he get my number? He must have been talking to my mom. Damn it. If she had known the history of us she would have not have given it to him. I couldn't be mad at her though as she was clueless to the situation.

Why, why, why couldn't he just leave it be? Our friendship was over years ago, I moved on, leave it be please! I had a feeling denying him would not be that easy. Seeing the loneliness on his face last night made me feel bad and I want to give in to him, at least hear him out, but I need to stick to my guns and say no. I text back Greg and told him I was doing better, but not 100%.

It was a lie that I was physically sick, but mentally I was feeling down and exhausted. He told me to feel better soon and that he would see me on Monday for my shift. Next up, I told my mom the same lie as Greg and she gave me the same motherly speech she always does when I'm sick. Rest up and lots of fluids.

She did confirm my initial thought that it was her that gave Ryan my cell phone number. Ryan told her that he got a new phone after he got out of rehab and lost his contacts and needed my number. Slick, real slick. She asked me to fill her in on what's going on with Ryan once we met up. What she didn't know is that I had no intention to talk with him.

I needed the company and I so badly wanted to meet up with Jake, but I needed to keep a low profile to avoid seeing Ryan around town. Knowing Jake, he would also want to jump in bed for a few rounds and there was not one ounce of a sex drive in me right now. My damn mind was on Ryan. I couldn't be with in bed with Jake while having Ryan on my mind. I text him back with the same excuse that I was ill.

He texted back a bunch of sad and crying emoji's. Oh, brother. I was not going to respond back to Ryan's text. Giving him a dose of his own medicine was just what he needed. How does that feel Ryan Black?

Being ignored by someone you care about is torture. Karma sucks my friend. Trying to keep my mind of his presence in town was not going to be as easy. I was curious to see what he had to say to me or how he wanted to make it up, but I couldn't, nor did I want to give in that easily.

Netflix binge sounded good. It could keep me occupied for hours. I finished watching the first season of *13 Reasons Why*. I watched the last five episodes of it and for each episode I watched I got a text from Ryan. Each time he begged me to meet up with him.

"Give me a half hour. C'mon I'm begging you. Please let me make it up to you."

The same text each hour and he said he wasn't going to stop until I gave into him. It felt good to see him beg like this. Each time he texted I giggled to myself. Not because I was giddy over the attention, but because it felt good to be the torturer this time. I do not see myself as a vengeful person at all.

It pains me to see others sad, in pain or hopeless, but this time I felt okay about it. Ryan cut deep when he shunned me and I didn't want to make it easy on him. It wasn't like I was physically or verbally abusing him or anything. Just throwing out what he handed me. Silence.

By 3:00pm he was now texting me every half hour. It was only Saturday and I was becoming bored being shacked up in my apartment. One can only read so many books and binge watch so many shows before you start to go stir crazy. Not sure I can make it another full 24 hours like this. Right on cue 3:30pm he sent another text.

"Give me a half hour. C'mon I'm begging you. Please let me make it up to you."

The kid is persistent I will give him that. He's becoming increasingly more persistent as the day goes on. I would imagine he would be on a fifteen-minute texting schedule by dinner. I hate this, I hate this, I hate this. I'm going to do it.

I'm going to give into temptation ONLY, because I want to get this over with and be done. Be done with him (again) and get back to my life. My life that was going good, I had everything that I could ever ask for; a good job, a good home, good health, a great family, a substantial amount in my savings and a decent sex life. I don't need anyone coming into my life and throwing what I have going for a loop.

Letting him vent, talk or whatever he thinks he needs to say to me will get him off my back. I will let him talk and try to keep the peace and kindly let him know I'm not interested in what he's offering, but thank you kindly. Saying that to him will work, right? It's going to be a piece of cake. Out of my life just as quickly as he decided to come back in. Boom done!

"You have a half hour and that's it. Meet me in an hour at Goodbye Blue Monday." I text him back.

"Half hour is all I need. Thank you for giving me a chance."

I'm indecisive about what to be feeling right now, not just about meeting with him, but everything. Should I be excited? Sad and depressed? Or should I let 100% of the anger take over my body, showing no compassion or kindness whatsoever? Angry is not who I am.

Granted I might be angry for a few hours, few days or at most a few weeks, but never do I let that kind of negativity take over who I am. The situation with Ryan was a bit different in the department of being angry. It took longer than a few weeks to get over that one, but only because we have so much history there. A perfectly good friendship went down the ol' shitter. Kindness and forgiveness are key components in my life.

There is that saying that fits this situation, "You may forgive, but you might never forget." Yes, this fits my situation quite well. My guard is up primarily because of the unexpected to come and feeling nervous above all else. Nervous to get hurt again, nervous for what he's going to say, nervous he's going to ask me to let him back in, nervous I will say yes to him no matter how much my mind is telling me no because Ryan has and always will be my weakness. I'm going to conjure up all the fight I have in me to stand my ground.

Butterflies have invaded my stomach. Between the excited butterflies and flaming nerves that have worked up a nervous gag reflex I'm not sure which of these was worse. Why was I getting so worked up? It's Ryan. He's not a complete stranger except as of recent.

I spent so much time on the couch pondering how I was going to act, what I was or was not going to say I know only had fifteen minutes to change and get there. If I'm a little late so be it. He can wait just like he made me wait. Bumming in my pajamas I needed to quickly change into some sort of acceptable public outfit. I was not about to get all dolled up for him, but I didn't want to look like a mopey slob either.

I put on favorite pair of skinny jeans, a loose fitting black t-shirt, a causal necklace, my green Converse shoes and called it good. Goodbye Blue Monday Coffeehouse was only a few blocks from my apartment so it would take me all of five minutes to walk there. We have been going to this coffeehouse since we were kids. I loved it; it had such a retro, cozy, artistic vibe to it. Keys-check, phone-check, nerves-check. My mind was in a complete fuzzy state. It couldn't keep up with itself; bombarded with all the possible scenarios that could take place during coffee talk with Ryan.

Looking down at my phone for the time I was only about seven minutes late. Ryan is clearly not worried that I wouldn't show otherwise he would have called me by now wondering where I was at. As I approached the coffeehouse door I stopped before opening it, closed my eyes and took a couple of deep breaths. Under my breath I repeatedly murmured,

"You can do this, you can do this, you can do this."

Feeling as prepped as one could for meeting up with your handsome, long lost best guy friend I walked through the door towards where Ryan was sitting with confidence. He was sitting towards the back of the store, near the wall with his favorite drink, caramel macchiato and mine, a white chocolate mocha. He saw me coming towards him and gave me a smile. He stood up like he was going to hug me, but I sat down before he could.

"So what is it that you needed to talk about, Ryan?" I said impatiently.

This should be good I thought to myself while I took a drink of my mocha.

"Right to it, I guess." He said still smiling.

Oh, come on. He had to expect some sass and sarcasm from me. It's only right. I will try not to lay it on to thick and be somewhat civil. He deserved a lot more than sarcasm and sass, BUT being the nice northern gal that I am and knowing what he has recently been through I will dial it down just enough to let him know, he was in the wrong.

"First off, how are you? How's life treating you?"

"Really!? You only have a half hour and you want to start off with small talk? If it were me I would get straight to business and make better use of the short amount of time I have. But that's just me. Life is good, I am good, my family is good. What other brain busters do you have?"

"Fair enough. I'm going to be in town for a while and I thought we could hang out and catch up with one another. We could catch a Twins game, hit up some breweries, do some hiking."

"Let me get this straight. You thought after five years of ignoring me, never returning my calls, texts or emails that we could just pick up where we left off when we were friends? Do you really, expect me to go anywhere with you, just the two of us to hang out? Ryan, I do not even know who you are anymore. Gathering from the pieces I have seen, off and on, on TV and in magazines, you have not been in a good place."

I felt bad bringing this up, but it's the truth. I do not know who he is. The Ryan I once knew would have not treated his best friend the way he did after he left, the Ryan I knew would have never got into drugs or put others in harm's way. For all I know he's a complete, snobby creep now.

"Ashley, I know I have a lot of making up to do with you. The way I ended our friendship and cut you off was wrong. Yes, what you have seen in the media was true, I got into a bad place in life and I worked hard on fixing me while in rehab. But I'm still the same person you knew growing up. That part of me has not changed. The final stage of my treatment was to come back home to relax, work on having a simpler, less stressful life and build back up the relationships that I damaged over the course of the last few years. That means you. I need you back in my life."

He seemed to be telling the genuine truth. In the past I could call his bullshit and right now I was not smelling any. Feeling another layer of defense start to melt away I snapped myself out of my daze. As much as I want to believe he wants to make things right I can't give in to him. I worked too hard to get over him and didn't want to chance reliving that hurt and disappointment again. Now to let him down.

"That is great you are back on track and trying to make things right. I'm happy for you. Really, I am, but I'm good right now with the people that are in my life and the life that I'm living. Letting you back in is no longer an option. I'm flattered that you thought of me and you want to be friends again, but I'm going to pass on that for right now."

"Please Ashley, please, please let me make it up to you."

"No, really I'm good."

Before Ryan could object to my denial, Jake walked up to our table. Cheese and rice, of all people to see right now. Is this happening to me? The guy I screw around with and the man I once was in love with. Can we say uncomfortable.

There was no reason to feel uncomfortable as Jake had no clue who Ryan was and vice versa. I didn't owe either of them an explanation.

"Hey Ash, where did you disappear to last night?" he said smiling at me.

Clearly, he was not worried about the guy I was having coffee with. That's what I loved about our "relationship", no strings attached. Ryan did look intrigued though and kept looking between the two of us, as if he was wanting me to introduce him to Jake.

"I had to bail early. My stomach was pretty queasy as the night went on so Greg let me go home."

Feeling anxious about the current company together. I couldn't wait for Jake to leave so I could get through this talk with Ryan.

"Jake, this is Ryan an old friend from high school." They started shaking hands as I made introductions.

"Ryan this is Jake. Jake is my friend from The Northern Lights band that was playing at the pub last night."

"Oh, yeah man. You guys had some great songs on your play list." Ryan said.

"Thanks. Hey, do I know you from somewhere?" Jake asked.

That was my cue to jump in and end the get to know you chat. Before Ryan could get a word out I said,

"Nope, not possible. Ryan is from out of town and just here for a quick visit. You wouldn't know him from anywhere. Anyway, how about I call you later and maybe we can go out for a drink?" I said hastily, hoping that he would get the point and move on.

I felt Ryan's eyes on me as I made plans with Jake right in front of him. My suggestion to call him later worked, he smiled and said,

"It was nice meeting you Ryan. Cheers." Raised his coffee to us and walked out.

I didn't want to explain Jake to Ryan nor did I need to. Who I make plans with is not a concern of his. We need to get back to business and get this over with. I didn't even give Ryan a chance to think long enough to come up with a question to ask. As soon as I saw Jake out the door I turned back to Ryan.

"What was it that you were saying?"

"I understand why you are hesitant and you have every right to be, but just think of all the good memories we had together and all the new great ones we can have."

"Ryan, please I just can't. I do not want to put myself in that position again."

I could feel myself starting to get worked up and with him begging me with those deep dark eyes- that draw me in every time-I do not know how much longer I would last before I lost it.

"What position is that?", he asked.

What I wanted to say is the position of loving you again, but I didn't want to drag that awkward conversation into this. That's what got us here in the first place.

"The position of us getting to know what another, becoming friends again, you returning to California to only put me on the backburner again. Let's just skip all of it please."

"Ashley, I need to tell you that there hasn't been a day that I haven't thought about graduation night and what you said…", as soon as he mentioned graduation night I jumped up out of my seat and cut him off.

That is not a memory I want to think about or talk about with him. I'm not going to be drawn back into that.

"Whelp, enough of that. Your half hour is up. It was really nice seeing you again and I wish you all the best in the rest of your recovery."

My abrupt goodbye and escape had turned a few heads and Ryan started looking nervously around at the attention I had caused. I grabbed my phone and key off the table and charged out as fast as I could.

"Wait, Ashley, please!"

I heard him call out behind me, but I just kept on walking and didn't look back. Now he knows how it feels to call out for someone and have them never look back. Briskly walking back to my apartment, I couldn't help but, replay our conversation back. Was he telling the truth-did he really, think about graduation night every day? Why?

If he felt the same way about me, if that is where the conversation was headed, then why did he leave me? Why did he shut me out completely? Whatever, this is the last time I'm going to think about it and I'm not going to dwell on it. I told him as nicely as possible I'm not interested and now I'm getting back to me.

17

The remainder of the weekend I did not hear one word from Ryan. He was respecting my wishes not to see him. When he said, he wanted to reconnect he had seemed so serious. It never used to be in his character to give up so easily but, I didn't know that person any more. People grow and change sometimes not for the better.

I meant what I said to him that I wish him luck in his recovery. No matter how bad he hurt me in the past I would never want to see him hurting.

Normally on Sunday afternoons I will go over to my mom's house to hang out with her and Charlie and have a family dinner together but, earlier that day I convinced her we should change it up and go out for dinner. Obviously, I had ulterior motives with this suggestion; avoiding bumping into Ryan. Which more than likely would have happened since his parents live right next store to mom's house. Instead we spent the afternoon hiking the trails at Carleton College arboretum, showered up afterwards and then the three of us enjoyed the warm summer evening eating some fresh pizza at my pizza place in town, The Red Barn Farm. Mr. Simon, my old boss was there working that night so it was nice to catch up with him.

I had not seen him since that year I put in my notice. Sitting at one of the outdoor picnic tables, eating our pepperoni and sausage pizza with a cold Blue Moon in hand was so relaxing.

"Hey, did you hear Ryan is back in town?" she said.

"Um, yeah, I knew. Sorry I forgot to mention it to you, but he stopped by the bar Friday night for a drink and to say hi."

Hoping she was not going to ask to many more questions about him.

"Oh, really!? A big star like that visiting my girl, I'm surprised you didn't tell me and all of Instagram. I mean he is your best friend. No harm in bragging, right?!"

Hearing her talk about him, she seemed a little star struck herself. I started to get a little anxious talking about his bar visit. Plus, I have no intentions to tell her I saw him again yesterday. Intentionally leaving out this tidbit of information was like lying to her. I hated being in this position.

"I think he kind of wanted to keep a low profile. He sat in the back booth where no one could see him. Making a big deal of his presence around a bunch of drunk girls I'm sure was the last thing he wanted mom."

"You are probably right. Well, what did he have to say? How's he doing since rehab?"

"Not really sure. To be honest it was loud in there from the band and I was super busy bartending. We didn't have a lot of time to talk. Just some quick small talk."

I kept looking down at my pizza to avoid making eye contact with her. I felt like if she locked me into her gaze I would break and tell her everything.

"Are you two getting together soon? It's been years hasn't it since you have seen him. What did you guys decide to do?" she asked.

Oh, my gosh, she just keeps going with the questions. I began to feel a little annoyed. It's not her fault by any means, she didn't know the real situation behind us, but I needed to find a way to end this conversation.

"We didn't really have time to make any plans. He said he would call me when he gets settled in."

"That nice honey. You two will figure something out. Tell that young man that Charlie and I said hi and he better stop in soon."

Charlie chimed in excitedly, "Do you think he will give me his autograph? Oh, my gosh he just has to. All the girls in school would love me if I brought that in."

"You will just have to ask him if you see him. He loves you Charlie. I bet he would walk around the halls with you. Bump you up to ultimate status in school."

"Cool!" he said in a day dream state.

Yikes, I hope I didn't get this kids hopes up. Ryan couldn't make things up to me, but he certainly could make Charlie's dreams come true. His social status would sky rocket especially with the ladies. Hope he doesn't let him down. We finished up our dinner and went our separate ways home.

Such a relaxing day now to top it off with a Sunday movie. As I plopped down on the couch to start a movie I heard my phone ding. It was from Ryan.

"Hi. Coffee in the morning? Let's say 8:30am?"

How premature of me to assume telling Ryan no thanks I don't want to be friends again would get him off my back. This was the Ryan I knew. Doesn't give up until he gets what he wants. Sorry you hounding me is not going to make me give up and give in. Nice try.

I didn't text him back and turned off my phone. That will shut him up, well at least until I turn my phone back on.

18

When I walked back into work Monday afternoon, I went straight to Greg's office to apologize for walking out on him on the busiest night of the pub's history. He's such a kind understanding man. Any other boss would have said don't bother coming back.

"You do not need to apologize Ashley. You are one of my hardest working employees, you never ask for days off, you show up on time and work your ass off when you are here. Today is a new day and I'm glad you are back. I just hope everything is okay?"

"Of course everything is all good. Sorry again for putting you through that."

"Oh go on now. Get back to work." He chuckled and waved me out of his office.

I was so happy to be back at work. It was a beautiful day outside; all the pub doors were open to let the light breeze come through and my favorite part about having the doors open was you could hear the rushing water from the Canon River outside. It was such a peaceful sound. The Minnesota Twins were also playing today and we always have the games on in the bar which was a perk because being an avid Twins fan, I didn't like to miss any of their games. I was confident they would pull off a win today. It was going to be a great day!

It was such a productive day at work so far. I got done with most of my check list so helped some of my co-workers out with their stuff. I didn't mind at all helping others out doing their jobs, as I like to stay busy at work. It makes the shift go by so much faster. As I was power washing the deck I heard Greg holler for me from his office.

Walking towards Greg's office I hollered back to him as I entered the office doorway. "Ya, Greg, what do you need?"

I stopped dead in my tracks when I got to his office.

"What are you doing here?"

Ryan was sitting there on top of Greg's desk so comfortably and Greg didn't seem to mind. They were acting like they had known each other for years and were catching up. Did Greg even know who this was sitting next to him? Greg smiling up at me from his desk chair swung around and said to me,

"Ryan here was just telling me you two have been best friends since the fifth grade."

"Something like that." I said glaring at Ryan.

"This young lad has come all the way from California to take you to the Twins game today."

They smiled at each other like they were in cahoots with each other and had this all planned.

"Oh, bummer for you I work tonight. Sorry, maybe next time you're in town." I said robotically to show my lack of enthusiasm for his dumb plan.

How dare he come to my work, again, and try to swindle Greg into letting me off for a Twins game. Did he honestly think even if he convinced my boss to let me off that I would willingly go with him? What about our conversation on Saturday, did he not comprehend any of it? If Greg even knew the half of it, he would have told Ryan to take a hike the moment he walked in the door. I turned to walk out of the office, but Greg got up teetering after me, Ryan smiling behind him thinking he had won the battle,

"Wait just a minute young lady. Your movie star best friend, came all this way to hang out with you and gosh darn it you are going to hang out with him."

Ah-ha! There it is! That's how he did, he named dropped himself. Apparently, being star struck is a real thing. I did not pin Greg to be the type to give a shit about celebrities. How desperate can one be to name drop yourself? Such a douche bag.

Then Greg bent over to whisper to me, "Plus, we made a deal if I let you off he has fourth row seats behind home plate for the rest of the season?"

I was shocked and flattered at the same time. Ryan really, wants to hang out with me. Guaranteed those tickets cost a fortune and then to give them to my boss just to let me off for the afternoon. Is this kid for real? I looked down at Greg smiling and nodding his head yes at me, like he was a little kid waiting for his mom to give him the okay to pick out a toy.

I looked over Greg's shoulder throwing daggers at Ryan. He knew he had me cornered and he knew I was too nice to say no to my boss.

"Fine", I growled, and stomped by Greg, right past Ryan and out the back door.

I was going to the game, but not happily. Initiation of conversations will be met with silence, jokes will not be met with giggles, but eye roles, drinking beers and saying cheers-not so much, sharing a tub of popcorn-not in this universe. I got into what I assumed was his black Jeep Grand Cherokee and as he jumped in after me.

"Here, this is for you. You should be supporting by sporting your local team." as he threw a navy Twins t-shirt at me.

"Look I know you think you have won, but you haven't. I still mean what I said on Saturday.

We need to keep our separate ways. This is only happening right now because I couldn't let Greg down. This is all for him and in no way, is it for you. Got it!?"

"Loud and clear.", he said smiling at me. "Let's listen to some goodies on our way up to the game.", he said as he started up a playlist on his phone.

He didn't seem worried, hurt or offended by anything I said. He seems confident that this little plan of his is going to work. As we drove up to the cities for the game he tried several times to make small talk with me. His questions were met with shoulder shrugs, ah-huh's and mmmm hmms. I looked out the window most of the ride up, humming along to the songs that were playing when I was not half responding to his questions.

During the few moments of silence we had in the car, I would find myself glancing over at him when he was not looking. For the supposed drug addict that he had been branded with he didn't look like one. Most addicts you see on the news or in media were gaunt and sickly looking, a sack of skin hanging off your bones. He posed none of the above. He looked healthy and still toned, had a lighter tan he brought back from California, still sporting his black hair that was now in slicked back look and he wore a five o'clock shadow-which I'll admit I like.

Just as he was before; tall, dark, handsome and now a rugged side to him with his stubble. What was a forty-five-minute car ride seemed like two hours. As we arrived near Target Field he started to look for the closest parking ramp possible. We found a lot about two blocks away. As we started walking to the stadium, he threw the Twins t-shirt at me.

"Don't forget this."

"Gee, thanks.", I said catching it.

"Are you going to attempt to enjoy the game. I know deep down being here excites you. You love this team more than anything."

"I will decide once we get in there. No guarantees that fun will be had. But, yes you are right, I do love the Twins."

"Once you put on the shirt, it will give you super human powers that will allow you to enjoy this day. You just wait and see."

I smirked down at my feet as we entered the stadium. This beautiful outdoor stadium was the best investment our state made. Anywhere you sat gave you an amazing view of the city skyline under a blanket of stars on a clear night. Although, I'm a country girl at heart there is something about the skyscrapers, lights and noise that take your breath away all while watching this great American sport. This may sound cliché, but hearing the crack of the bat from hitting the ball was my favorite sound in the world.

Hearing it brought back so many good memories of my dad and I playing baseball in the backyard. Sometimes when I hear that sound I can close my eyes and see that image clear as day. As if I was in that very moment from so long ago. I went into the nearest bathroom to change my shirt. I hated that I was wearing this gift from him.

I wanted nothing from him at all, but wearing it was justifiable as I didn't want to look out of place and it was only right that I support the home team by wearing their merchandise. As I walked out of the bathroom, Ryan was waiting there for me and commented,

"See, was that so hard."

Ryan led us to our seats. He entered the section 9-I couldn't believe it, then we started walking to our row-past row M, L, K, J, H, we finally stopped at row D. Holy shit row D! How in the frickety frack did he manage these seats? Never in my life did I dream I would sit four rows behind home plate. Never!

These must have been the same seats he offered up to Greg. Greg is going shit when he sees where he is sitting. It was hard to contain my smile as Ryan held out his arm to gesture I enter the row first. He knew he had me at section 9. Damn this kid.

My guard had melted a little more and there was no way to avoid it at this point. He knows what baseball means to me, the history I have with it, the love of the game. Just as we sat down the game had begun. The Kansas City Royals were up to bat first. I was not concerned about ordering a beer or other concessions.

The moment I sat in my seat I was engrossed in the game, more than normal. These seats had me in a deep trance I couldn't be awakened from. If Ryan tried talking to me during the first half of the game I didn't know. During intermission, I finally came to and looked over at Ryan. He was just sitting there smiling at me.

"Welcome back.", he said chuckling.

"What?!", I laughed back.

I knew that I hadn't been a good companion, but I was not here for companionship or to have a good time with friends so to speak.

"You were out of it for a quite a while. It's fun to watch how excited you get during the game."

"Well, that's what we are here for is to watch the game, right!?"

"Yep. How do you like these seats?"

I looked at him and rolled my eyes, "Oh stop it, you know these are amazing seats."

I couldn't believe what I was about to say, but it was the right thing to do regardless of my original feelings about this whole day. This experience has meant the world to me and it's not likely I will ever sit in seats like this again.

Looking him in the eyes I turned to him and said, "Thank you, Ryan."

"Of course, not a problem."

"No, really, I mean it. Thank you. You do not know how much this means to me."

"Yes, I do. It's the least I can do for you considering my past actions."

I wish he didn't bring up our past at all. It just brings me back to the reality of what was which brings me down. I turned back around in my seat to face the field.

"Only the best for my best friend.", he said.

Enough of the best friend talk; I needed to walk. I jumped up from my seat and Ryan looked up at me.

"Bathroom, I will be back." I needed to breathe for a moment.

As angry as I was earlier today about coming here with Ryan I found myself enjoying it. He meant well by his actions and what was it hurting? It was going against everything that I promised myself that I wouldn't do. I wouldn't become his friend, I wouldn't enjoy his company, I wouldn't have a friendly conversation. I admit it is nice having him back and there was a part of me that did want to hear what he had been through in California.

I had lacked close friendships at home since Brooke and Ryan left years ago and it would be nice to have that back. It couldn't hurt to get to know one another again and build back a friendship that once was so wonderful. That's what he wanted too, right!? I decided in that moment that it was okay to let my guard down little by little, to slowly let him in one day at a time. Walking back to my seat I could feel the stress lessen.

This decision was a good one. Holding grudges against someone was a lot of work and feeling heavily guarded all the time sucked the life right out of me. As I got back to our row I sat down next to Ryan and smiled at him.

"What?", he said warily. Looking at me like I might say or do something crazy.

"How about a beer?"

Surprised by my suggestion he said, "Oh, hell yeah. Lets' get you a beer."

This was pleasantly one of the best days I had in a long time. Once I got over my stubbornness, deciding to let loose and give him a chance the day became quite relaxing and fun. We spent the remainder of the game not talking about the past, but enjoying each other's company and living in the moment; drinking, corn dogs, people watching and a great ball game. It was turning out to be a great start to my week.

The Twins won 8 – 5. The night couldn't have ended any better. As we left Target Field Ryan suggested we stop across the way for a beer before we went home. Thinking to myself that we best be on our way home and not ruin the good night we have going with drunken conversations, that need not be had. Alcohol being a truth serum would only bring out thoughts, words or actions that no one, including Ryan wants to see from me.

The mood during the car ride home was a 360 from the ride up there. We rocked out to the radio and talked about the night. As we pulled into the parking lot of my apartment building we sat in silence for a few minutes before we started to say our goodbyes.

"Thanks again Ryan for this amazing night. It was a lot of fun."

"I had a lot of fun too. Thank you for unwillingly coming with me today. Truly, this is all I wanted, was to get an audience with you somewhere, anywhere and hang out like we used to."

"Well, thanks again.", I said as I started to open the door.

"Maybe, I can come up and we can hang out some more and catch up. The game wasn't really the place to talk considering we had to shout to hear each other."

"Sorry, I'm going to call it a night. I work tomorrow afternoon and I should probably get some sleep considering it is already way past my bedtime. Good night."

I climbed out and as I was about to shut the door he called after me, "I'll call you tomorrow."

He is persistent, he wasn't going to give up on building Ryan and Ashley back up. You know what, I'm okay with it.

19

Time flies when you are having fun or so they say. A month and a half had past and Ryan was still here in Northfield. It's like we picked up right where we left off, like nothing had ever changed between us. I had no idea when he was going back home to California nor did I want to ask him. I'm just embracing the time that he's here with me now and not thinking about the future.

We are in such a good place right now and I know it will stay good even when he does leave. It was like we were in an episode of *Leave It to Beaver*. Everyone around me including myself was in a fantastic mood and always smiling. Golly gee whiz things were going swell. Joking aside it has been a great summer so far.

The Blacks' were happy to have their son back and were looking lively again compared to when I saw them in the pub that day. At work, the pub has been busier than ever. Sales have doubled since last summer so needless to say business is booming for Greg and his wife. I haven't seen the smile leave his face since the day Ryan gave him those season tickets to the Twins game. Not to exclude mom and Charlie either.

Mom took a new job with the school district as Health Services Director which allowed her to be home nights and weekends and for the first time since dad's death she has a new boyfriend. Charlie was excelling in baseball this summer. In July, we received news from Brooke that her boyfriend Tom had proposed. They were coming home in a few weeks and getting married here at home. I found it odd that they didn't want to get married out in California considering that is where they lived.

Tom doesn't have a big family and the few of them that there was, were okay to fly out to Minnesota for the occasion. Since the two of them travelled a lot with their acroyoga group they didn't have a lot of time to plan a big wedding. She was a simple, laid back girl and didn't want a big fancy wedding. The only important thing to her about the planning was it be at home in Minnesota surrounded by her family and close friends at The Red Barn. Brooke, had her mom plan everything for her which was not to too big of a task considering they were having about 100 people attend.

She booked the barn, picked out a simple menu of chicken breasts, mashed potatoes and green beans. They were not going to have a wedding party either since this was all happening a month from the time they got engaged. Whatever floats their boat. If they were happy. I couldn't wait for her to come home.

Although, I have always been in contact with Brooke by phone or Facetime I hadn't physically been face to face with her since graduation night. I couldn't wait to give that girl a hug and I suppose meeting the main man in her life was a big deal too. Not to sound selfish or intentionally leave anyone out, but I'm hoping in the short time she is home she can sneak away for an afternoon to come hang out with Ryan and I. Like old times. Ryan was doing exactly what he said he would, making up for lost time.

We did everything under the sun together and more. We went to my brother's ball games to cheer him on, hiking, movies, beach days, Twins game-this time as I normally would be sitting in the nose bleeds which is just as good to me-going out for drinks, apps and dinners sometimes. Nights that I worked, he would come visit and drink. We would hang out at my apartment or my mom's house with her and her boyfriend. We even resumed having Sunday night barbeques with both of our families.

This is the happiest I had been in years. It felt so good to have this breath of fresh air in my life. As weird as it sounds, when Jake came to town, the three of us even hung out together. Of course, I never divulged to Ryan what kind of relationship I had with Jake. I can't imagine Ryan hasn't figured it out by now.

I still like what I have with Jake when he is in town and the bedroom activities didn't stop just because Ryan was home. I still flirted, hugged and touched him even when Ryan was in our presence. I was not intentionally trying to make Ryan jealous when Jake was around, but I sensed that was his mood when we were all together. He always looked uncomfortable when I would get too touchy feely with Jake, or he would make up an excuse to get up or leave. I don't know why he didn't try to pick up a lady friend for the night too.

I didn't care if he did and wouldn't stop him if that's what he wanted. Maybe it was because he didn't have a place to bring them back to. He could always suggest their place if they had one. Ryan and I were just as he said, friends. There was no reason to cease doing what I had been doing with Jake.

It was the last weekend in July, Jake and the band had left to go back to Nashville. Ryan text me that Sunday morning telling me he had a surprise for me and would pick me up around 8:00pm. I was excited to have some Ryan time tonight since I had spent the whole weekend with Jake. I'm curiously eager to see what he has in store.

I text him, “What should I wear for your surprise?”

“Casual. I will mention that the surprise is in the outdoors so dress accordingly.”

A surprise outdoors, at night? I had no clue what it could be. Maybe he discovered a new outdoor brewery that had an amazing patio. I loved when new breweries opened. We talked about someday visiting every brewery in the state of Minnesota.

It will take a while, but I know we can do it, one brewery at a time. I decided on a cute little burgundy romper and a black cardigan in case it got chilly. Not likely for a night in July, but I’m bringing it with anyway. I threw on some makeup and a few loose, beach curls.

Casual, but cute. A little before 8:00pm I heard my phone ding. Ryan, letting me know he was out in the parking lot whenever I was ready. Giddy for my surprise and to see Ryan, I sprinted out the door. In the rush of my excitement I might have even forgot to lock the door.

Settling into the car, I didn’t even great him with a hello. My investigation began,

“So Mr. Black, where are you taking me?”

“Well, Ms. Monroe, you are looking more beautiful than the last time I saw you!”

I felt myself blushing. I was not used to him calling me beautiful in a serious manner. Felt good to hear it from him though.

“Thanks, you don’t look too bad yourself. Now tell me where are we going? I’m dying to know.”

“If I told you then it wouldn’t be a surprise. We aren’t going far so you can ponder the surprise for a few more minutes until we get there.”

He was enjoying this I could tell. The smile had not left his face since he picked me up. I was baffled as to what this surprise was going to be since we weren't going far. Ugh, I used up a cute outfit for a surprise in town. It can't be that good if we are not even leaving city limits.

My excitement was muted a bit. As we drove through town to wherever it was we were going I thought it was a good time to catch up on my Instagram feed. We didn't talk much on the way to our destination, but I didn't think too much about the lack of conversation. After about five minutes of scrolling I glanced out the window and began to recognize the surroundings. We were by the Carleton College campus.

Up the hill to my right was some of the main classroom buildings, to my left was the football field, immediately after that was the soccer fields. Soccer fields meant we were going to The Grove. He turned into the matted grass path that led to the parking for The Grove. It was a little unnerving being back here. The both of us had not been back here since that night and we all know how that ended.

The last memory I had here was filled with sadness that was followed by greater upset and sadness. The past is the past, think positive Ashley. The positive memories made in this field irrefutably outweighed the negative ones and that's what I need to zero in on. Maybe there was some party he heard about out here and thought it would be fun to relive those days of high school one last time. The gesture was nice and I would go along with it and enjoy the night with my best friend.

We pulled into the empty parking lot that was also a field. We were the only car here. My guess was wrong, there was not a party. So, what were the two of us going to do out here?

"The Grove? There's no one else here, no party?", stating the obvious.

"C'mon you'll see." He smiled as he got out of the car.

Unnerving was now an understatement. The feelings in my stomach were atrocious. The entirety of what was my intestinal track was now in double sheel bend knots and shrunk up into my throat. It was one thing to be here with other people surrounded, but another to be here alone with Ryan. What was waiting for me in The Grove?

I might not make the walk to The Grove. My medical history would not show you any history of anxiety, but in this very moment it's present and if someone doesn't hand me a brown paper bag now I'm going to faint right here and now. He grabbed my hand and led the way to the walking path in the woods. Thirty feet into walking is where the bridge over the creek stands. Eek, the bridge is in desperate need of updating.

The boards were all old and rickety and some were popping up from their once screwed down state. I pulled Ryan back a bit implying I didn't want to cross. I would rather cross through the creek and being soaked the rest of the night then risk tetanus from a slice of one of those rusty nails.

"She's still sturdy, I promise.", he said reassuringly sensing my hesitation to cross.

As I crossed the bridge I concentrated on the peacefulness the sound of the running creek water brought. It helped me to cross the bridge and brought my anxiousness down a few levels. Nature is medicine. I swear by that statement. Still holding my hand, we came upon the opening to the grove.

A bonfire. A bonfire is all that stood in this space.

"What's this?" I asked him as we walked towards the fire.

"Yes, this is the surprise. A warm summer night, stars, a field of memories, our favorite activity-sitting by the bonfire here in this place with my girl."

Whoa, his girl? What did he mean by this? His best friend yes, but that was it. We sat down on one of the logs by the fire and adjusted our rears to get comfy. It was an amazing spot I'll give him that.

We sat there in silence for what seemed like ions. The silence between us was met with singing frogs, chirping crickets and the crackling of the fire. He seemed nervous the moment we sat down and I couldn't figure out what his deal was. What he said next caught me off guard and never in a million years did I expect.

"I don't think I ever really told you why I came home, did I?"

"No you haven't. Tell me bestie, why did you come home?"

"Coming home was the last step in my treatment process."

This was the first time he had ever brought up rehab and his trouble from back in California. I had an inkling that this conversation was going to turn serious.

"Oh, really!? Why did they feel you coming home would help your problem?"

"The alcoholism and prescription drugs were a lot worse than the media knew about. To remove myself from the problem I needed to completely uproot myself from Hollywood, my friends and job out there. Everywhere you turn, no matter how hard you try to avoid it, those temptations were always around; movie premiere parties, on set, colleague's houses, the bars, the beaches. There is no way to escape it, not unless you leave. My therapist in rehab highly recommended this move back home and tasked me with allowing myself to give into what I really wanted and struggled with for years, but never allowed myself to have it."

He seemed distraught as he was telling me this, like a beaten down dog. I was feeling bad about being so anxious.

"Well I agree with your therapist. Give yourself what you need if it means helping you get better. If it's something I can help you with let me know man, I'm here for you. So, what is it that you want, but struggled to have in life, with all your movie star money that could buy you anything?"

"You."

"What do you mean me? I'm here for you, aren't I?"

"I want the you that confessed your feelings to your best friend almost five years ago in this very spot."

"What? I…I…I…", stuttering to get my words out.

Frozen from shock like the night he came back into my life at the pub. I don't understand what he's asking of me.

"I'm sorry I don't understand?"

"That night, five years ago when you confessed and then we kissed. That kiss scared me. It scared me because it made me realize there was a part of me that felt the same way. In that moment, I looked and felt for you in a different way than I ever had. I was leaving, you were staying and I didn't think a relationship beyond friendship was something I wanted. After that night, there wasn't a day that I didn't think about that kiss and you. Each day passed and I found myself wanting to be with you even more. But, I was angry at the timing of it all. I made all these big plans for my future and wanted to give my life a go out here. I was confused on what to do and struggled with what to do about it or how to act on it. I knew the only way to make it easier on myself was to cut you out of my life. Believe me, it was hard, letting you go like that. I didn't mean to hurt you, but I didn't know of any other way. It haunted me every day the way I treated you, it angered me that I couldn't be with you because I was out here being selfish."

"Stop.", I said to him.

I didn't want to hear any more. It was too much. The thought of all these years we could have stayed friends or even fallen in love.

"When my therapist demanded I come back home to reconnect with what was positive in my life before I left home. The one and only positive I could think of was you. I knew coming back here was going to be hard and even harder was deciding if I wanted to throw your life out of whack by coming back. I was nervous and scared to see you and what you might say when you saw me. Seeing you in the pub that night was a sensation I can't describe. But watching you work, seeing you then and now it only confirmed that I loved you then and I love you now and I want to be with you. I don't want to lose you again."

My eyes were starting to well up, but I continued to stare straight in the fire. There was a conglomerate of mixed emotions and thoughts running rampant in me right now. I was in no state to sort them out now or saying anything back to Ryan. I said all I could say to him in the moment. I pleaded with one word as my tears quietly started to spill over onto my fire warm kissed face.

"Stop."

"I'm sorry Ashley, but I needed to tell you. You deserved to know."

I stood up, still looking into the fire crying.

"Please just take me home."

I shut down. This is not what I expected; this was not what I wanted to happen. We were so happy being the friends we once were. Why, Ryan, why did you have to drop this bombshell on me now? Things have been going amazing for us.

Deep down I knew I felt the same way. I had worked so hard to keep those feelings buried, but these past few weeks we have been so happy together. Had I been so happy because I had unknowingly let those feelings free? Had I been using Jake as a cover up when Ryan was around? When the three of us were together I knew, it bothered Ryan and I knew his jealousy was driving me.

The car ride back to my apartment was silent. My mind, frozen in shock, from what Ryan had just confessed. I stood staring straight out the windshield and the only thought I had was that I couldn't wait to be home. Who would have thought the tables would have turned, the same feelings revealed, in the same place, but by the other party? As soon as his car hit the parking lot of my apartment I squeaked out a quick good-bye, jolted quickly out of the car and ran up to my apartment where I crashed into my bed crying.

20

Ryan's confession left me feeling confused and indecisive. I didn't know what I should do about it, if anything. I wasn't sure if I truly was feeling the same way about him now as I did five years ago. I felt like there was something there or was there really? Was my mind trying to convince me that I was still in love with him?

The friendship I wanted back so badly I did get back, but those intimate feelings I once had for Ryan-that he now admits to having - I wasn't sure if I was feeling them again as well. I had boar them deep down in the depths of my heart that I made sure it was nearly impossible for them to resurface. My mind and my heart were fighting to figure out what was true. Just like the bad timing of my confession five years ago it now holds true with Ryan's confession now. Brooke and her fiancé were set to be home this Wednesday for their wedding this weekend.

I didn't have time to even sort out something like this. Two days wasn't enough time to sort through years-worth of feelings, love and friendship. I should be thinking about planning a last-minute bachelorette party for my girlfriend, the three of us hanging out somewhere, what I'm going to wear to the wedding, but now the fun in that is dampened by what I want with Ryan. Ryan has been sweet about the whole thing and has called me repeatedly, telling me that he doesn't expect anything to come of his confession and he just wants to know that I'm okay, how am I feeling about all this.

What I wanted to say to him was, *how do you think I'm feeling? I loved you for years in that way and never being able to have you like that, only to have to move on from it and now you throw at me that you feel the same and always have. Yes, Ryan, the answer is so simple…not!*

I had avoided seeing him since Sunday night after he brought me home, even though he begged and begged to see me so we could talk. Each time he asked I made up an excuse that I was busy washing my hair or shopping for something to wear to the wedding. By Tuesday afternoon, I requested that he drop it for now and give me some space, that we needed to concentrate on our friend Brooke and her weekend of happiness. Surprisingly, he obliged. I had not heard from him since Tuesday afternoon and it was now Wednesday.

It wasn't even twenty-four hours since we last spoke, but it was a big deal considering since Sunday night he was calling or texting me every few hours. There was no avoiding him completely like I wanted to, as Brooke had arranged for all of us to meet up at Froggy Bottom's River Pub for an informal engagement party. It was more of an excuse for all of us friends to get together before the chaos of the wedding started in on Friday; with the rehearsal, groom's dinner and the big day itself. Hopefully, Ryan could keep hush, hush about everything tonight since we would be around a group of old and new friends.

"I'm home!", Brooke text me.

"Can't wait to see you. I can't believe it's been five years. I miss you so much!", I replied back.

"I miss you too. You better be ready to get your drink on girl! It's long overdue."

"You bet I'm ready. We missed each other's twenty-first birthdays. We have a lot to make up for."

"Ha, ha damn right we do. I'm excited for you to meet Tom. You are going to love him."

"Any man you love, I'm going to love too. I'm so happy and excited for the both of you."

"Thanks hun. I wish there was time for just the two of us to talk. We have years of gossip to catch up on."

That we do, I thought to myself.

"Well, my trip out to California is about five-years overdue so maybe this fall if, when you have some down time I could come out for a long weekend visit?"

"I would love that Ashley! Now that I am a seasoned Californian I can show you anything and everything out there."

"Sounds like we got ourselves a girl's weekend planned." I said elatedly.

"Fantastic! By the way, have you heard from Ryan? Is he coming tonight?"

"I saw him over the weekend and he never mentioned one way or another. Why wouldn't he come, he has nothing to better to do. No Hollywood premieres or parties to attend."

"Has he talked to you at all about what happened? How is he doing with recovery?"

"He has been pretty hush, hush about it all. Not sure if he feels embarrassed or if it's too hard to talk about? As far as I can tell he's been doing phenomenal."

"Such a relief to hear that. You hear so often about addicts relapsing. I just feel terrible I was not around for him."

"Don't feel bad. You both were leading your own lives out there and from the sounds of it rarely saw each other anymore."

"Yeah, but I still feel bad. Okay, enough of the Debbie downer talk. Have a pep talk with your liver and we will see you tonight."

"Ha, ha sounds good. See you then."

The engagement party was still five hours away and it was clear that this was going to be an all-nighter. Not confident I could pull off an all-nighter I was going to power through it for her but, to do so I needed a nap. I made sure to set my alarm on my phone because I guarantee with how emotionally and mentally exhausted I have been I could sleep through the rest of the day. If I'm awake by 5:30pm that will still give me plenty of time to make a quick dinner and get ready. Feeling refreshed after my nap I was ready to go and take on the night and the alcohol.

I was not sure what to wear to an engagement party so I went with a tight olive green skirt, flowy white tank top, flats and coordinating gold jewelry. Back when I was in school I used to hate getting dressed up and putting on makeup, but now I didn't mind it. I now looked forward to the times where I could get out of my leggings and t-shirts. The pub we were meeting at was directly across from The Contented Cow on the other side of the river. It was not even a walking block away.

I literally had to take a few steps from my apartment building, walk over the walking bridge and down the street. No sober cab needed. You couldn't ask for a better setup for a night of drinking. There was a 70% chance of a thunderstorm this evening so I grabbed my umbrella since I would be walking. Rain could put a damper on sitting out on the deck at the pub, but I love a good thunderstorm.

It brings a sort of calm and I LOVE sleeping with my bedroom window open when it's raining. I left it open so the smell of rain can envelope my whole apartment. It was 8:00pm on the dot so I made my way out to the pub. As I walked across the bridge towards Froggy's, I noticed Ryan was already out on the deck with a few people I didn't recognize. They must have been friends from California.

I hope he doesn't notice me walking over so he won't feel inclined to come indoors. The less I have to be around him the better. I have not seen him since Sunday night and with everything being out in the open between us I don't know how to act around him since I haven't got my shit sorted out. I walked into Froggy's front door and walked down the historical spiral staircase that their bar was known for. As cool as it was to have something like this in a bar, it was a bitch to walk up when you were tipsy trying to leave.

I swear Brooke knows my scent or something as I was not even half way down the stairs and she began gleefully screaming my name, ran over to me and about knocked me down with the biggest hug ever. We both cried happy tears of joy to see each other. She grabbed my hand and led me over to a table they had near the patio doors to meet her fiancé Tom. He was not the tall, dark and handsome type that I was attracted to, but he was still good looking. Tom was about 5'8"-not too much taller than Brooke, blonde hair, but shaved almost to the scalp, but impressively built.

When I say built I do not mean body builder style where there is too much muscle-it was a healthy, attractive build. As Brooke, introduced us I couldn't help observe how glowingly she looked at him; even though she was talking to me she couldn't take her eyes off him. The whole thing was adorable-how cute they were together, the love and adorer shin for each other. Seeing what they had together made me realize how I longed for something like that. It was lonely not having that someone to look at me that way every day and worship the ground I walked on.

Giving up on love years ago, even at my young age, I realized I had convinced myself I would never have it. I would never have it because I didn't want it without Ryan. I glanced out the patio doors through the window at Ryan sitting there drinking and laughing with his buddies outside. He still didn't notice I was here. Ryan said he felt that way about me, but it's hard for me to trust him still.

Knowing the playboy that he was in high school and still was a few months ago; I couldn't trust he wouldn't get bored with me, or want a younger version of me, most of all there was the fear that if I let myself go, to fall in love with him again that he would leave me. Leave me lonely and broken hearted. Abandonment issues are ever present in my life and with good reason. I think there is even a name for what I have- Athazagoraphobia. Fear of being forgotten, ignored, or abandoned is a real thing. I Googled it to be sure.

Why did I even need to know that useless information? I don't need to know that, I just looked it up one day for shits and giggles when I was feeling down. I made the rounds with Brooke to meet all her California friends, Tom's family that flew out here and there was even a few old classmates from high school that showed. It was interesting to hear what everyone had been up to since high school. As promised I did a few shots with the bride to be.

After the second shot, I thanked God when someone had pulled her away to talk. Taking shots has never been my thing. I have always been a beer girl. I took a seat at the bar and ordered myself a Blue Moon. It was smooth going to down the hatch pipe.

The smoother beers go down the faster you drink and get drunk. Sounds like a good plan to me-getting drunk. It would help me forget my loneliness at least for a few hours. It was nice sitting there by myself for a while just singing along to whatever songs were playing overhead. Dwelling in my loneliness and predicament, drinking my Blue Moon, I heard the start of my favorite country singer on the radio-Miranda Lambert.

Her new single "Pushin' Time" was the sweetest little ditty. I was in love with it, as I was most of her songs. Her lyrics were so raw, real and relatable. As I was humming the song to myself I heard his deep voice ask me,

"Dance with me?"

"What? No. This isn't a dancehall, it's a bar."

Looking around there was actually a few other couples dancing, but regardless I didn't want to be close to him and still was not up for talking to him. He then pulled me off the stool and walked me over to some random open space,

"We are dancing, it will be fun."

I didn't have the energy to argue with him, so I gave into his demand. He grabbed my waist and pulled me in close. We didn't talk to each other, just danced. Swaying back and forth to Miranda's song, I breathed him in. Ryan's smell was always so intoxicating and still is.

I never thought to ask him what brand of cologne he wears, but I do know that he has kept with the same brand as he wore in high school. It was probably Abercrombie and Fitch; that seemed to be what all the boys in school wore back in the day. They say smells can jog memories and that it did. It brought back the memory of the first time I realized I loved him, all the good times we have had together and even the bad, our first kiss vividly flashed across my eyes, Sunday night's confession and then I felt it.

The flutters in my stomach and pounding of my heart. Being this close to him, in his arms, his hand on the small of my back holding me close, the sides of our faces touching. I pulled back just enough to look him in the eye. We stared at each other for a moment. I was falling and falling fast.

Again, with the water works, I was on the verge of crying. I didn't want to cry in front of him or anyone else there. I broke from his embrace, grabbed my purse off the bar and ran as fast as I could up the stairs, leaving him standing where we danced. Crying in front of an audience meant explaining what you were feeling and why. I sure as hell was not about to do that and that's my reasoning for my abrupt exit from one of my best friend's engagement party.

It was pouring rain outside and having left my umbrella back at the bar I was in for my second shower of the night. It was useless to go back and get it as from the moment I stepped outside the pounding rain had made it look like I had jumped in the Cannon River. I made a run for it before anyone else besides Ryan would notice I'm gone. Just as I ran back over the walking bridge I heard Ryan yelling behind me.

"Ashley!", he tried yelling over the rain.

I pretended not to hear him and kept running. As I kept on running I knew he was still behind me because he was still yelling my name. He finally caught up to me and grabbed my arm to stop and turn me around to face him.

"Why did you run out like that? Are you okay?"

We both were soaked. Even squinting we could barely look at each other without our eyes getting pelted by the rain drops. I didn't know what to say to him, I didn't want to tell him that I was falling for him again, even though it's what he would want to hear. I tried to just pull away so I could keep walking towards my building, but he grabbed my hand again to hold me from leaving. He wasn't listening to me, which turned to irritation and then I blew it.

"I can't do this with you Ryan."

"Do what? What did I do?"

"Be this close to you, be around you all the time, I'm going down the path I don't want to walk again. I'm falling…."

He didn't let me tell him the words he had been waiting to hear; that I was falling for him again. He didn't hear them because he grabbed the backside of my head to pull me in to kiss me. His full lips and soft kiss, it felt so right. It was exactly like the first time we kissed, but better. Better this time around because all feelings were now mutual.

I didn't want it to end and….it didn't. The physical chemistry between had overtaken the both of us. It had been busting at the seams to break loose for so long. The threads were weak and they gave way. I do not know how we made it to the walking tunnel that led to my building door, but we had.

The next thing I knew he had me pushed up against the brick wall, passionately making out and rubbing against each other. It was new, intense, different, something I couldn't find in my other lovers, a dream that was on repeat, for so long and now becoming reality. Unlocking lips long enough to ask if he wanted to come up to my apartment. Saying nothing back, he confirmed what we both were wanting by flashing me that melt me smile of his, nodded yes and kissed me again. We sprinted up the stairs to my door.

Being all hot and bothered in my current situation made it impossible for my trembling fingers to hold the key steady enough to unlock doors. I stupidly dropped it a few times before success. I was nervous and excited all at the same time and we couldn't get into my apartment fast enough. As soon as the sound of the deadbolt unlocking reached the tiny hairs on our ears, he spun me back around, pulled my waist into his. He reached behind me to open the door all while still kissing me.

The door whipped open and we stumbled inside, he slammed the door behind him and for a moment we both just stood there, breathing heavily, looking at each other in the dark shadows of my apartment. My entire being was on fire and pulsating for him. He lunged towards me and brought me in close to only begin passionately kiss me again. Every so often he would slip his tongue onto my lips and barely into my mouth. It was what teased my senses and made me want more of him.

From outside in the rain to the living room of my apartment there was all of ten minutes that we weren't locked in at the face. Still in an embrace we made our way down the hallway towards the bedroom. About half way down he stopped and stepped back from me and swiftly took off his shirt and threw it to the ground. What he hid underneath those shirts everyday was gorgeous, he was toned in all areas of his upper body, he had dark chest hair that trickled down to his abdomen area, but it wasn't thick enough to cover his slightly tone six pack. Not at all the clean shaven upper body I imagined, but nevertheless it turned me on, he turned me on.

We had not turned on the lights when we came inside, but that did not matter as there was enough lighting from the storm striking often enough that we could see each other. The darkness intertwined with the periods of lighting and thunder made this night even more erotic. Not wanting him to feel like a lone duck, I slipped off my white, soaked shirt over my drenched, dripping hair and tossed it to the floor. I reached back to unsnap my bra and letting it drop to my feet. He stared intently at my bare breasts and after a moment snapped back to the task at hand. Me.

He grabbed and lifted me up by my bottom and pushed me against the wall. Kissing and nibbling at my neck line, groping my breast with his left hand and holding me up with his right. No one has ever touched me or kissed me in the way Ryan was doing at this very moment, it was rough, but sensual at the same time. I caught myself moaning a little. He carried me back to the room my legs tightly wrapped around his torso.

He set me down on the floor and we simultaneously grabbed for each other's pants. In one shot I unbuttoned his jeans; Ryan in one swipe dropped my skirt and undies to the ground. He sat down on the bed and pulled me on top of him. Grinding on each other's rain soaked bodies was immediate, the lighting, thunder and stormy breeze from my open bedroom window made things steamier. As I arched my back, he continued kissing every part he could reach.

Picking me up again, he threw me onto my back and took over. He felt so good to me and I let him know it. The friction, groping, kissing, the passion was so intense. The beginning, middle and end were better than a sex scene you see in a movie. It was better than any past experiences I had.

Being in that moment with someone you hold so close to your heart, the one we have loved all along heightens things to a new level. At least it did for me.

21

I awoke to the ding of a text alert. Ryan's arm was still flung around me and he was cuddling up to my back. I rubbed the sleep out of my eye, picked up my phone from the night stand.

"Ryan, get up! You have to go now!"

Urgently shouting at him as I pulled on some dirty clothes of mine I had laying on the floor. Startling him awake from jolting out of bed, he threw the blanket of his still naked body and jumped out of bed.

"Why? What's happening?"

"My mom, she just texted me and is five minutes away from walking through my door. She can't see you here this early. She will know something is up. Please get dressed in the next 30 seconds and go!"

"Really!? You want me to go after what happened last night. Ashley, she will find out about us eventually. Just tell her now."

He was nakedly trying to convince me to do something I wasn't ready for. My irritation at his procrastination began to rise quickly. I couldn't just drop the ball on my mom that Ryan had feelings for me and wanted to be together. That's not something you can drop and leave someone with, especially my mom. That would require morning coffee and a few hours of details.

Last night was unbelievable, but waking up this morning I realized I was still unsure if I wanted us to stick. Basing my future with Ryan off, of last night was not a responsible way to decide what I wanted. Thinking back on last night now freaked me out. How could I let myself get caught up in the heat of the moment? Leading Ryan on is not what I want to do to him.

It wouldn't be fair to the both of us. I need to rationally think things through. Frantically running through to pick up our damp clothes off the floor, I threw mine in the bathroom hamper and tossed his at his face.

"Go, Ryan, now! Please she is going to be here any minute. I promise I will call you later."

"Okay, okay!" he said defeated.

I had him dressed and out the door within the first three minutes of my mom's text. Now all I can do is pray that they don't bump into each other as he leaves and she arrives. If it came to that and she asks questions I will have an excuse ready as to why he was here so early. Something like, *he was bringing my umbrella back*. While I waited for my mom to get here I washed my face, put my hair up, made the bed to hide any evidence that sexual encounters had occurred here last night and made a pot of coffee.

Five minutes had passed and she still was not here. Sitting down on the couch, under my favorite grey, chunky knit blanket and closed my eyes. Episodes of last night flashed behind my eye lids. Feeling disappointed in myself for last night's moment of weakness.

Longing for a relationship, the engagement party, Ryan's confession, and my physical attraction to him all lead to that moment last night. I had talked myself into allowing it, without thinking about how it would mess with the both of our heads and feelings the days after. Two days was nowhere near long enough to sort through years of feelings, moments and whether I truly wanted to give into a future with the man I have always loved. Most importantly to me the chance of risking reliving the pain of five years ago should he decide to ever leave me, again.

The moment my mom knocked, Ryan texted me, *About last night,* with the winking emoji. Ugh! Rolling my eyes and tossing my phone on the kitchen counter. Letting my mother in and putting on the best happy act that I could. Now that my mom worked at the school district she had summers off. It was nice to see her more often now.

"Good morning! How's my girl doing this morning?"

"Rough, it was a long night last night."

"Good thing I brought you hangover reinforcements. Your favorite-white chocolate mocha."

"Thanks, mom you're the best!"

It was not even worth telling her that I was not hung over, but tired at this point was feeling about the same as a hangover.

"Tell me how last night went? How's our little Brooke doing? Is she a glowing bride? What's her fiancé like?"

"Mom, mom, calm down. You will get to see them both Saturday. But yes, she is glowing, happier than I have ever seen her and Tom seems great. They make a cute couple."

"Aw, that's so sweet."

"Yeah, it is."

"So I didn't stop by just to bring you coffee, but to see if you would come with your old lady to find something to wear for the wedding? My fancy wear is a little dated."

"Ha ha, yes of course I will. Are you thinking of going up to the Mall of America?"

"Considering I do not dress up often, there is no need to spend an exorbitant amount of money on a dress. Target, will do just fine don't you think?"

"Target is great. They always have cute summer dresses."

"Target it is! Now get dressed and let's go."

What started out as a quick trip to Target, turned into a full-blown girls' day. We found mom a dress for Saturday, manicures and pedicures and ended with lunch. I needed this time with her so much. While we were eating lunch Ryan text me again, *Can I stop by later?* I informed him that I was not home and left it at that.

He questioned back when I would be home. Not ready to see him again and not wanting to explain to him why I didn't reply. Seeing him would only complicate things; leading him on and not allowing my head to think. My mom dropped me back off at my place and I spent the next few hours tidying up my apartment. After the cleaning was caught up, the rest of the day was for me.

I needed time for me, to collect myself, take care of my mind and body and figure out what to do about Ryan. I sat in a hot bubble bath for almost an hour, in silence, in my thoughts. What do I do about Ryan? What we shared last night was incredible. I loved every second of it, I loved all of him, I loved our connection, but the regret I felt this morning is still fresh.

It only complicates my decision to be with him, to give him that chance that he never gave me five years ago. I do love him, that is clear now more than ever, but the wounds from the past are too vivid. They brought on a pain and a fear that I don't want to feel again. That fear has taken over my life one to many times already. Twice is the amount of times I have felt it consume me, it was too much to bare.

I'm not ready to risk fear devouring my life once again. We can't be together like he wants, like I want. I will tell him Saturday at the wedding. It's not the ideal location or time to tell him that kind of news, but my past has proven I'm not good with the timing of anything. I've made up my mind and it is final.

He's not going to persuade me to change my mind. I can tell my heart is already in deeper than it should be because I can feel it tearing. Damn it! After my not so relaxing bath, I jumped into bed. It was time to mope and have a good cry.

A good cry always seemed to help the stress subside and calm me down.

Knock, knock, knock! Ryan was at my door, uninvited, asking for me to let him in.

"Ashley, it's me Ryan. Let me in if you are home. We need to talk."

Those were two things that I didn't need in my state of emotional distress; let Ryan in and talk about last night.

"Ashley, please. Let's talk. I know you want to."

Knock, knock, knock, again. The best course for me right now is to ignore him. Being face to face with him will only bring back that weakness and I need to be strong. My decision is what is right and best for me. As hard as it was I stayed in my bed not moving.

Eventually he stopped knocking and left. Being as persistent as he has been the past few weeks, he then began to call and text me. I turned off my phone to resist the temptation to respond and laid there staring at the ceiling. I had to keep repeating to myself over and over; *you are strong, you will be okay, this is what's right*. After a few hundred times of repeating this I drifted off to sleep.

Thank heavens I did because I needed this day to end.

22

Wedding day was here. My best friend gets to marry the love of her life and I couldn't be happier for her. I was so excited to share this day with her, her family and friends. Wedding festivities, the dance and food were something I always looked forward to especially at The Red Barn Farm. It was a magical place to get married at.

All day Friday, Ryan did not yield in trying to contact me. He stopped by again that morning knocking on my door for a good fifteen minutes. Every few hours he would text and call, but I held strong and did not answer the door or my phone. I was feeling sad and broken, but I just kept repeating the words to myself; *you are strong, you will be okay, this is what's right.* Saying this helped resist my urge to falter.

By 4:00pm, it was becoming increasingly hard to resist. Reading his texts were chiseling away at me. *Can we talk? Did I do something wrong? Why are you ignoring me? Please give this a chance.*

I put my phone on silent and turned off the vibrate option so that I wouldn't hear the phone calls or text messages come through. I left my phone in my room and stayed as far away from it as I could. I set the oven timer in the kitchen so I knew when it was time to get ready for the night. Traditional wedding ceremonies start in the early afternoons, but they wanted a sunset ceremony so Brooke wouldn't walk down the aisle until almost 8:15pm tonight. Ryan would be at the wedding too and there would be no way to avoid him then.

I was nervous to see him. My plan was to tell him everything tonight, but I was feeling quite cowardly about doing it. My plan was to arrive at about 8:10 and sit towards the back so that he wouldn't see me, at least not right away. At dinner time and reception, I planned to try and surround myself with friends and family or just always be talking with someone so he couldn't get me cornered and ask me what was wrong. That would work, right? Doubt it.

I opted to wear a tight fitting, little, black dress that accentuated my curvy hips more than I liked it to. The night was going to be warm and I didn't want to be sweaty the entire night so I put my hair up into what I call the "librarian's bun." To make my legs not look like stubs I put on some black heels. Dressing up like this made me feel pretty. I deserved to feel pretty.

It was about 7:45pm and would take me about fifteen minutes to get to the barn. I took my time walking about not only because I didn't want to roll an ankle in my heels, but I was in no hurry to get there early.

As I pulled into the gravel parking lot of my old job, I noticed the bride and her father were just lining up to walk down the aisle. They were starting things a little earlier than what I had planned. I was still there in time to see her walk down, but that meant as I was walking to my seat all heads would be turned towards the bride walking down the aisle. My tardiness would be noticed by all guests and I would be noticed by Ryan earlier than I wished, so much for that plan.

Not wanting to be the distraction that took a way from Brooke's moment I stood up by my car before I walked over to my seat. I could see her perfectly from where I stood and she looked beautiful! Tears of joy spilled over onto my perfected shimmering makeup. Hopefully, the water-resistant makeup holds up. As Brooke's dad was handing her over to Tom, I made my way to an open seat in the back row. Thankfully, no one noticed.

The happy couple couldn't have asked for better weather than this. It was a warm, summer night, a little on the humid side, yet not uncomfortable, the sky was clear with a few twinkling stars beginning to shine through, bright orange, red and yellow colors stretched over the horizon from the descending sun. A storybook sunset. Brooke and Tom began to say their vows to each other. Normally during this part of the ceremony, I'm crying again, but I was distracted.

Finding myself scanning faces and heads in the crowd of wedding gawkers for Ryan. I scanned it three times and didn't see him anywhere. It was odd that he wouldn't show for one of his best friend's big day. My actions better not be what are holding him back. He needs to look past that for the sake of his friendship with Brooke. I'm jumping to conclusions, but what other excuse could it be?

By the time I snapped out of my thoughts the bride and groom were kissing their first time as husband and wife. I stood up from my chair clapping and whistling for my friends. The recessional wedding music was played by a lone guitar player, "Marry you", by Bruno Mars. I loved it! I hadn't heard that one for a recessional song yet, but it was fitting.

Guests began to exit the rows and follow the happy couple out the aisle and back towards the bar where the remainder of the celebration would be held. Unsteadily in my heels, I worked my way up the small grass hill into the barn. The barn was decorated simply, but beautifully. Tables were covered with lace table cloths, each also having two little wood boxes that acted as a vase for the small bouquets of flowers. Mr. Simon had added three crystal chandeliers that hung from the barns ceiling.

It was still rustic, but added a touch of elegance. Right outside the barn was several lines string globe lights decorated the outside to add a little mood lighting right outside the barn. The whole night was romantic. By the time everyone gathered up in and around the barn for dinner and dancing the sky had turned to night, but heat had not yet left for the day. I made my way over to the bar and needing something a bit stronger than beer I ordered a Moscow mule.

As I sipped my drink from the cocktail straw, I scanned the crowd again for Ryan. Where in the hell was he? I should be relieved he didn't show. Bad news and drama averted. I wasn't relieved though. He needed to be here for Brooke.

What was going on between the two of us should not get in the way of supporting Brooke and her happy day. I began to worry. I checked my phone to see if perhaps he tried calling or texting me, but there was nothing there. Did ignoring him right after we hooked up set him off back into a deep abyss of depression? Was he in trouble? Was he looking for drugs?

I love him, but I just don't want to be in a relationship with him. Surely, other girls have done worse to him in California. I didn't think ignoring him would send him backwards. I felt myself getting upset. Being an emotional wreck already from the past few days it was easier for me to cry.

I used to rarely ever cry and now seeing a puppy on a commercial would get me teary eyed. I needed to go find him and make sure he was okay. Once I know that he is I will buck up and tell him that we can't. I was leaving my best friend's wedding to go search for my other best friend. I didn't want to ruin Brooke's night by telling her Ryan wasn't here and I was leaving so I left it be.

As soon as I found him I would come back anyway. She wouldn't even notice I was gone. I slammed my drink back down on the bar and ran towards the open barn doors. As soon as I exited the barn to bolt to my car, there he was, slowly walking up to the barn. His walk was a mopey one of sorts; both of his hands were in his pocket, he was dragging his feet as I could hear the shuffle of gravel as he took each step.

Man, did he look incredible though- heather grey dress pants, a white dress shirt and loosened black tie, hair slicked back. I have never seen him look as good as he did tonight. Our eyes met, he looked tired and defeated.

"Oh my gosh, where have you been? I was beginning to worry."

"Ashley, I…", he began to speak, but I immediately cut him off to scold him.

"Tell me, what was more important out there that you had to miss your best friend's wedding ceremony? I hope Brooke didn't notice you weren't there. She will be crushed. How…"

Then it was Ryan who cut me off.

"Ashley, stop!"

"Stop what?", I said with some guff.

"Stop fighting this. Stop fighting us. We are good together. Ignoring me is not going to make me go away. We are meant to be together. Sorry it took me so long to let get to this point; to allow myself to love you back the way you have loved me so long. I know I hurt you, I never meant to, but I'm never going to put you through that again."

His words stopped me in my tracks and sent a cold shiver down my spine. My right arm was covered in goosebumps and it wasn't even windy out. I grabbed it with my other arm to rub them away. Gazing around to see if there was an audience and thankfully it was just a few guests coming in and out of the barn, but no one stopping or gawking to hear what was unfolding. I couldn't get myself to look him in the eye so I stared at the ground.

I knew what I was going to say next was a lie and I'm not a good liar. In fact, when I lied my cheeks tended to blush. It was terrible to deal with. I couldn't even lie to a waiter at a restaurant if I thought the food was good or not when in fact it was lukewarm and tasteless. The only way I would be able to get it out was to not look at him.

Stay strong Ashley, you will be okay, this is what's right.

"Ryan, I just can't. I have moved on. We are just friends. I don't feel that way about you anymore. Please stop asking me to be with you. You are making this harder for me."

I looked up to see his reaction. He began walking towards me. The flutters arrived again and the melting began.

"If you do not have feelings for me than how am I making this harder on you? If you didn't share the same feelings that I feel for you then you wouldn't have allowed me to stay the the other night. You love me, I know it's there, you are just holding back. Why won't you let this happen?"

Feeling flustered by his questions I backed away from him a few steps. I could feel everything was going to boil over.

"You are going to leave me again after you are done with me or go back off to California to make your next big movie. Home is not good enough for you; you will get bored and leave me. I'm not good enough for you."

"Ashley, you are not some one night stand, you are not some temporary fling, you mean everything to me, you are my once in a lifetime. I'm never going to leave you again. I love you. Be with me."

That was it. That's all it took. I love you. Tears spilled down my face the moment he said it. As distraught as he looked walking up to the barn, to the calm way he talked to me, the way he never looked away from me even when I couldn't look at him, he was telling the truth.

I believed him now. He wouldn't leave me again. Even though I didn't say it in words, I knew the tears were a giveaway to him that I was all in. Grabbing my waist, he pulled me into him and kissed me. He kissed me gently, lovingly for what seemed like forever.

I didn't want this moment to end. It is the most romantic moment I ever experienced, under the glow of the string lights, in front of this old rustic barn, on this perfect summer night, with him, my always.

23

It's been a few months since that incredible night I made that decision to be with Ryan, to give into us. This is the happiest I have felt since before my dad died. Ryan has been incredible and things between us have never been more right. We went home that night together after Brooke's wedding and spent another glorious night together. It was just as steamy as the time before.

In fact, we didn't leave my apartment the whole next day. We were making up for lost time so to speak. This time I did not feel guilty about us or the night we had together again. When the guilt did not resurface, I knew that my mind and heart were in sync. With all the eyes and ears around us the night of the wedding it was only a matter of time before someone figured us out.

I thought no one was around, apparently, it was Brooke who noticed us "quarrelling" outside the barn and of course had to investigate why. She later told me she couldn't hear much of what we were saying-since we weren't shouting-but she saw Ryan kiss me. As soon as she saw this it was in a matter of ten minutes that the rest of the barn knew about it. I wasn't mad at her for telling everyone. It felt good to get it out in the open.

No more making up lies or excuses to cover up how we felt about each other. Brooke, feeling elated, told us that it was the best wedding gift she could have received-her two best friends in love. Both of our parents found out that night as well since they were guests at the wedding and both were shocked, but happy for us. Neither of them had any idea what had been going on between us. A few weeks later my mom demanded a coffee date to fill her in. It took a few hours.

In December, the both of us went out to California to move his stuff back to Minnesota. He was giving up all of it for us, for me. All the things he worked so hard for; the big fancy house, the Hollywood friends, the connections, the fame, the big paychecks, the warm weather! He told me he didn't need any of that or want any of it any more. It didn't mean anything to him because he didn't build it with me.

He filled out the paperwork to put his house on the market and hired an estate company to do an estate sale on most of his belongings. We were only bringing back a small moving truck full of his stuff back to my apartment. When he decided to re-root back to Northfield, I mentioned the idea of him living with me. He didn't even need to think about it, he just said yes.

Since Ryan was still working on his recovery as an addict, he took the next year off from doing any work, of any kind, he had enough money saved from his work in movies and television to make being unemployed and living comfortably work. When we weren't together he spent his time to his DAA meetings, mental and physical health. I'm inspired by his dedication to getting healthy again. Also, I'm happy to report he has not once relapsed. Acting is no longer in the cards for him as there is too many connections in that industry that might bring the temptation to relapse. Ryan set himself a goal, that when he is one year sober he wants to sit down and talk with Greg about buying out his bar. It would be a joint venture for us to do together.

Of course, our parents thought we were moving too fast and suggested Ryan should be in his own place for a year at least. That was crazy talk. We were not a new couple who didn't know each other. We have been friends since the fifth grade. We know the ins and outs of one another, likes and dislikes, wants and desires, hopes and dreams.

Nothing about this was rushing in, we were already pushing time. We finally got to be together in California like our original plan after graduation. This time we weren't staying. We were going to build our lives together in the place where they came together. We spent a week out there and stayed with Brooke and Tom.

It was nice to spend the time with them and see what Hollywood was about. We went and tackled the touristy stuff that I would have done if I would have moved out here; studio tours, beaches, Rodeo Drive, Beverly Hills, Hollywood Walk of Fame, restaurants, Hollywood sign and more.

In hindsight-things happened the way they did for a reason. It was just a long, painful, bumpy road in getting where we are today. If I would have moved out here things might not have worked out between Ryan and I. He wouldn't have had the time to stew in his feelings for me and come to the realization of how he felt. I might have found someone else out here.

The what ifs are endless. There is no use wasting the energy in thinking about those. I have the person I want to be with forever and always and I'm not looking back.

That first night he told me *I love you* I knew then he was serious about being together and I never once doubted him after that night. Ryan moving back to Minnesota only reconfirmed his commitment to us.

Made in the USA
Lexington, KY
01 September 2018